## "I vowed that I'd never be so impulsive again."

Aaron raised his eyebrows high enough they touched his bangs. Reaching up, he patted his head as if looking for something. Miriam frowned before she realized what he was searching for. His missing hat. The one waiting to be laundered to remove the splattered egg.

To her surprise, her lips twitched toward a smile. "Or at least I try not to be. At least not on the big things."

"So…no more *Englisch* parties."

"Definitely not." She emphatically shook her head.

"No more blue jeans?"

"Haven't worn them since."

"Purse?"

"*If* I carry one, it has a zipper and a strap."

"And I suppose you don't trust handsome and charming men anymore?"

She cocked her head in consideration. "I don't know. When I meet one, I'll see." This time she smiled as she looked up to meet his warm gaze. Something she never thought possible when reminded of that horrible night.

And she had Aaron Raber to thank for it. Something else she'd never thought possible.

*Publishers Weekly* bestselling author **Jocelyn McClay** grew up on an Iowa farm and ultimately pursued a degree in agriculture. She met her husband while weight lifting in a small town—he "spotted" her. After thirty years in business management, they moved to an acreage in southeastern Missouri to be closer to family when their oldest of three daughters made them grandparents. When not writing, she keeps busy grandparenting, hiking, biking, gardening, quilting, knitting and substitute teaching.

### Books by Jocelyn McClay

#### Love Inspired

*The Amish Bachelor's Choice*
*Amish Reckoning*
*Her Forbidden Amish Love*
*Their Surprise Amish Marriage*
*Their Unpredictable Path*
*Her Unlikely Amish Protector*

Visit the Author Profile page at LoveInspired.com.

# Her Unlikely Amish Protector

## Jocelyn McClay

LOVE INSPIRED
INSPIRATIONAL ROMANCE

# LOVE INSPIRED®
## INSPIRATIONAL ROMANCE

PLEASE RECYCLE

THIS PRODUCT IS RECYCLABLE

Recycling programs
for this product may
not exist in your area.

ISBN-13: 978-1-335-58620-9

Her Unlikely Amish Protector

For questions and comments about the quality of this book, please contact us
at CustomerService@Harlequin.com.

Love Inspired
22 Adelaide St. West, 41st Floor
Toronto, Ontario M5H 4E3, Canada
www.LoveInspired.com

Printed in U.S.A.

Judge not, that ye be not judged.
—*Matthew* 7:1

First and always, I thank God for this opportunity.
I thank Caren and others who graciously answered
my questions involving law enforcement.
Thank you for doing what you do.
Any mistakes are entirely mine.
And, Kevin, thank you for your continued patience.

# *Chapter One*

Why, of all the men in the district, or the state of Wisconsin for that matter, did they have to hire him? Plucking a wooden clothespin from the trio in her mouth, Miriam Schrock jabbed it over the wet sheet. Efficiently moving down the clothesline, she fastened another pin to the end of the bedding. Her narrow-eyed gaze slid again to the dark-haired man climbing onto the seat of the manure spreader parked next to the barn. Prompting the team of draft horses into motion, he directed the Percherons toward the gate of the snow-dusted field that bordered the yard where Miriam was working.

Bending down to the basket, Miriam shook out a towel and hung it on the parallel wire. *That is not your business. Just be glad they hired you.* Miriam wrinkled her nose in acknowledgment. She was glad, extremely so.

Particularly as, at age nineteen, she was a bit old for the role. But thankfully, this opportunity with the Zooks and their recently arrived *boppeli* had arisen just when her employment helping new mother Rachel Raber with her twins had come to an end.

She hissed in a breath as a brisk breeze whipped against her cotton skirt. In spite of the cold, she liked Wisconsin. Gathering another handful of clothespins, Miriam used one to secure a washcloth. *Enough to want to stay permanently?* Surprised at the ripple of temptation that swept through her, she sighed. Probably not. Her future was back in Ohio with Levi Peachy. Or so he'd finally hinted in his last letter.

Miriam paused, her hand resting on the pinned cloth. She should feel more satisfaction from the current missive. One of the reasons she'd come up north was to see if absence really did make the heart grow fonder. It seemed it had for Levi. She frowned at the energy that hummed within her. Was that longing? Or was it the realization of all she had to do today?

At least she'd been successful in her primary reason for coming up. She'd missed her *breider*. She hadn't seen Malachi, Samuel or Gideon since they'd moved to Miller's

Creek over two years ago. She'd even missed their big-brother teasing—to some extent. It certainly hadn't taken much persuasion this fall when Gideon had suggested she make the trip. She'd started working for the Rabers and their twins almost as soon as Gideon had picked her up at the bus station. And had enjoyed every minute of it.

Except, she recalled darkly, when *he'd* returned. Bending, she picked up one of her new charge's broadfall trousers. From its smaller size, Miriam surmised it belonged to six-year-old David and not eight-year-old Philip. In her bent position, she could see the black legs of the Percheron draft team from under the dangling sheet. Thankfully, the view of their driver was blocked. She jerked upright, trousers in hand. The man just irritated her. Because he reminded her of someone she'd rather forget? Someone responsible for the worst night of her life…

Willing the memory away, Miriam hung the pants and reached for another pair from the basket. Even in this diminutive size, belonging to two-year-old Abram, zippers weren't allowed so the pants had a broad flap that unfastened on the sides. With the addition of newborn Uri, there'd be even more pants to hang in the future. Smiling ruefully, she secured the miniature garment on the line. But by then, she wouldn't be here to see them.

Surely by that time, Levi would determine he had enough money saved for them to marry. It was what she wanted. Wasn't it? Miriam slapped the damp fabric in front of her to smooth out some of its wrinkles. It was what she *should* want at least. Of course it was. Levi was the most practical choice for her to marry of the men in her Ohio district. His cautious temperament was a *gut* balance for her more…impetuous nature.

Again recalling what her impetuous nature had gotten her into, Miriam flushed as red as the undergarments—the ones stuffed way in the back of her dresser drawer—that she'd purchased at an *Englisch* yard sale. Levi's more plodding disposition was a balance she needed. Scowling, she wrapped her chilly fingers around another handful of pins, which she again clenched in her teeth.

At the sound of a horse and buggy, she glanced toward the road. Although she didn't recognize the driver, she lifted a hand and returned their wave. *Gut* thing it wasn't one of her *breider*. If Samuel or Gideon caught sight of her now, they'd tease that they needed to keep clothespins on hand to deter her from talking. Although they'd also agree that while the obstacle would slow her down, it wouldn't stop her. Not from expressing her opinions anyway. Miriam plucked a pin and put it to use. *Ach*. She preferred their banter to Levi's reaction. He'd quietly—most times anyway—chide that her sentiments weren't necessary.

She grimaced. Right now, what was necessary was getting the laundry done, as there were numerous other tasks to address when that was finished. A household with seven children under the age of ten generated a lot of laundry, among other chores. The Raber house with only the two infants had been busy, but this one? Well, extreme busyness would keep her from thinking about the new hired man at least.

Besides, he didn't need her help on that. Aaron Raber thought enough of himself as it was.

While working for the Rabers, seeing him on the rare occasions he came to help his brother Ben had been bad enough. But to have to see him daily? Have to prepare meals for him? Sit across the table from him? She gave an exaggerated shudder.

It wasn't that he was a hardship to look at. And he knew it. Dark-haired and blue-eyed like his younger *bruder*, Miriam had heard more than one young woman sigh while her attention rested on the oldest Raber *bruder*, sitting with the other single men across the way on Church Sundays.

They'd only witnessed his charming side. Miriam huffed at the thought. Aaron Raber, charming? They hadn't seen him like she had, snarling at her sweet employer, Rachel, over a situation that'd been all his fault. The husband-seeking girls couldn't see past his outer shell to realize that the fellow, like one she'd known, would be nothing but trouble.

The draft team's harnesses jingled in the adjacent field. Miriam glared in their unseen driver's direction. She grabbed the last item in the basket. At least she wouldn't be doing *his* laundry.

At the splattering against the nearby sheet, a sound accompanied by a bitten-off exclamation, Miriam jerked her head up. Ducking the loaded clothesline, she looked toward the field where the draft team plodded just beyond the fence. The clothespins tumbled from her open mouth as she watched the manure spreader fling its contents against the freshly washed laundry. She shrieked. The driver hastily drew the team to a halt. Shifting a lever, he ceased the spinning at the back of the manure-laden wagon. Miriam stood frozen in outrage as he launched himself off the iron seat and cleared the wooden railings between them with a one-armed vault. Skidding to a halt in the low snow of the recent January thaw, he shot a glance at the now speckled laundry before spinning to face Miriam.

His mouth opened and closed a few times like he was going to say something—from which he wisely refrained. The strong column of his throat bobbed in a hard swallow above the top of his jacket. Following a gusty exhale, he shook his head as he gave her a crooked, sheepish smile.

"Sorry about that." When she didn't respond, only stared in return, he swept a look over her and continued, "Blond hair, red face, dark coat. You look like a version of Neapolitan ice cream." Aaron gave her a slow wink. "Only not so cool and refreshing." His smile slowly expanded into a grin, as if he was expecting her to share it.

Fragments of a snowball were dripping down his face before Miriam was even aware of scooping one up. "How's that for cool and refreshing? Because you look like the back end of the Percherons over there." She jerked her head in the direction of the stationary team. Hands as cold as her face was hot, she clenched them into fists before snapping her arms up to barricade her chest. Prepared for a missile fired in retaliation—no more than she deserved—Miriam's eyes narrowed when Aaron slowly shifted his stance and gave her his profile.

"What are you doing?"

"Turning the other cheek. Isn't that what we're supposed to do?"

Miriam hugged her arms more tightly against her. "I've heard you have a problem with that."

Aaron turned back to face her. One cheek bore an angry red mark. Raising a dark eyebrow, he made a show of brushing the remaining ice crystals from his face. Miriam winced at the unspoken comment on her ability to control her own temper. An all-too-accurate dart.

His mouth wearing a cynical curve, Aaron folded his arms across his own broad chest and shook his head. "I'm sure you've heard a lot of other negative things about me as well."

Miriam bit her lower lip. She had. She'd gobbled up the rumors like a pig at a trough as they'd reinforced her own unfavorable opinion of the man. Having him acknowledge it twisted her stomach with guilt. "Your words. Not mine."

His smirk softened to a crooked smile.

"Your words are written all over your face. They'd scare the chickens a week off having eggs if they could see them."

"Well, they're safe for the moment, as it will be some time before I can get to them with all the laundry I have to redo now."

Wincing, Aaron dropped his arms and glanced at the clothesline. Miriam was surprised to glimpse real regret in his blue eyes. When he spoke, his words were a quiet murmur. "Can I help you pull them down?"

*"Nee."* She nodded to the waiting horses that'd turned their huge black heads toward the yard and were watching curiously. "You need to get back to the team. You've got work to do." She flicked her gaze toward the soiled laundry. "So do I." Turning her back on him, Miriam jerked the clothespins off the wire to toss them into their container with an angry clatter. Feeling the weight of his gaze, she hunched her shoulders. When she heard the crunch of hesitant footsteps on the snow, she looked over in time to see Aaron exit the yard. With a scowl, Miriam gingerly returned the now soiled laundry to the previously emptied basket.

She hadn't liked the man before she'd spoken with him. And he certainly hadn't improved upon closer acquaintance.

* * *

Aaron ponderously crossed the wooden fence bordering the field and strode to the patiently waiting Percherons. The way she'd glowered at him, he felt like the contents in the wagon behind them. Climbing onto the cold metal seat, he picked up the lines and immediately directed the team diagonally into the field. This time, he made certain the wagon cleared the edge of the yard before releasing the lever to start the spreader again.

With a shoulder-lifting sigh, Aaron watched the young woman in the yard strip the now dirty laundry off the clotheslines. Even in her agitation, she displayed the same grace of movement as when she'd hung the wash a short while ago. He should know. He'd watched her from the moment she stepped out the side door with the basket tucked under her arm.

It hadn't been a trial to do so. She walked with a confidence that reminded him she had three older *breider* and she probably held her own with all of them. At the same time. Now, having been on the receiving end of a glacial blue glare, he was sure she did. When he'd first seen her, he hadn't paid much attention. He was too absorbed in confronting the girl whom for years he'd thought he'd marry.

A girl—*nee*, a woman—who'd become the *mamm* of not one child, but twins, in the months he'd been away. Months in which he'd agonized over whether to marry her as everyone assumed or set her free so she could find someone who'd love her as she deserved to be loved. Love her as a beau and not how he'd realized he felt toward her, as a brother. Marriage for the Amish was for life. They didn't believe in divorce. Once you were wed, there was no changing your mind.

It hadn't been his best moment. Aaron grimaced as he turned the team to make another pass of the field. There'd been several moments that hadn't been his finest since he'd returned home a few months ago. No wonder the glare-with-the-blond-hair didn't think much of him. He hadn't thought much of himself lately.

Well, at least one of the reasons he'd left the community for the *Englisch* had been resolved. Determining Rachel was a wonderful girl and didn't deserve the way he'd treated her, he'd come back to Miller's Creek to sacrifice himself on the altar of matrimony, only to discover his sacrifice wasn't necessary. His *bruder* Ben had already married her. The couple seemed extremely happy together.

And not only wasn't his sacrifice needed—

for the most part, neither was he. Nothing had been going right since he came back. There was no interest in the gasoline and diesel motor repair business he'd dreamed of starting, making the skills he'd honed during his time in the *Englisch* world pointless. There *was* a need in the community. Aaron knew there was. With connection to electrical grid not allowed in the district, too many things ran on motors and generators for there not to be. But it seemed the Plain folk would rather take their repairs to the *Englisch* shops instead of support one of their own getting started. At least, as long as he was that one.

Maybe they doubted he was going to stay around. He was. At least he hoped to. Aaron rubbed his hand over his face, wincing as he encountered the area where her snowball had connected. He'd stay as long as the other problem he'd left to avoid didn't get out of hand. A storm cloud had been rising in that area as well. He should've known. He'd been a fool to get involved in that situation in the first place. Bile coated the back of Aaron's throat as the ending phrases of the prayer he'd been taught as a boy—one spoken often by the Amish— seemed etched on the big horse collars of the draft team in front of him. *And lead us not into temptation, but deliver us from evil.*

Temptation hadn't needed to lead. Like a fool, he'd trotted up right beside it.

And that was it right there. He'd been a fool in a lot of ways before he left. An arrogant fool to boot. Full of himself and a lot of...

At the change of sound in clatter behind him, Aaron looked over his shoulder to see the spreader was empty. Shifting the lever to stop the spinning, he slumped on the seat as he directed the team toward the barn.

That's what folks probably remembered. Why they weren't giving him much of a chance. They remembered the fool he'd been. The one who'd left his well-respected folks without a word. The one who'd basically abandoned his longtime girlfriend at the altar. The one who'd driven too fast, whether it be a buggy or any automobile he'd managed to get behind the wheel of. The one who couldn't be relied upon, whose younger *bruder* had had to quietly come behind and make things right. The one who'd been rumored to use his fists a time or two when Amish believed in nonresistance.

At the lengthy list, Aaron pressed his lips into a thin line. Those were all solid reasons for the community to be wary of him. And why he'd been more than relieved when Isaiah Zook had offered him a job. His hands tightened on the lines as the Percherons headed eagerly for the barn. But no one knew the worst of it—the main reason besides his turmoil over Rachel that he'd left the area for most of the last year. Or at least Aaron didn't think they did. He squeezed his eyes closed. *And lead us not into temptation, but deliver us from evil.*

It was better the district didn't know. It needed to stay that way. Opening his eyes to glance toward the yard, Aaron found the clothesline now empty. Miriam, full laundry basket propped on her hip, was marching up to the house. He sighed as he guided the draft horses through the gate.

If it didn't stay that way, then everyone in the community would have the same opinion of him as the woman who'd just shut the door with a finality that cut across the cold winter air.

# Chapter Two

The sound of the opening door, followed closely by the aroma of cattle, announced the men had come in from milking. Miriam kept her attention on the food she was dishing up from the stove. She'd been trying to forget about Aaron Raber all day. It'd been particularly difficult while redoing the laundry.

The task could've been completed faster, but Joanne, the Zooks' youngest daughter, had wanted to help. Although her aid slowed down the process, Miriam hadn't been able to deny the little girl's request. That was how they learned. The girl had been more help than the gas-powered washing machine. Although Isaiah had purchased the machine when the twins, now six, were born, it wasn't currently working. So while Miriam had cast longing glances at it, the clothes needing to be rewashed had been scrubbed instead using more manual methods.

"What happened to your face?"

Miriam stiffened at Esther Zook's question. Turning to see the men finish hanging their hats on the pegs just inside the door, her attention zeroed in on the one who'd never been far from her thoughts—her dark ones anyway—all day.

"Oh, this?"

Her eyes rounded as Aaron touched the red blotch on his face as if he was unaware of its existence. She sucked in a breath when his gaze settled upon her. He was still carrying the mark of her hurled snowball? She'd hit him that hard? *Oh help!* Her own cheeks reddened with embarrassment as she braced herself for him to blab about what she'd done. It was no more than she deserved for firing the missile at him anyway. She hadn't worked for the Zooks that long. Would they keep her on when they heard of her actions? She was supposed to be an example for the children. A *gut* one, not... Miriam hissed in a breath when Aaron, still holding her gaze, gave a slanted smile.

"One of the cows caught me with her tail. Must've had rocks in it, the way it felt when she swatted me." Even as he voiced the explanation—possible, but far from true—his eyes told Miriam he knew exactly what she was thinking.

*"Ach."* Esther winced sympathetically from where she sat with her newborn son in the nearby rocking chair. "I've been the recipient of that many times before myself. Do you want to put anything on it to make it feel better?"

"Hmm." Cocking his head, Aaron stroked his beardless chin as if in deep consideration. "I've always heard a kiss would make things better. Maybe from the one who caused it?" His gaze remained on Miriam. The one-sided smile bloomed into a full-born grin, matched by a provoking gleam in his eyes. Miriam's face heated more than it did while canning over a hot stove during the dog days of summer. Her fingers curled around the edge of the steaming bowl of potatoes, instantly wishing she could trade the contents for another snowball. Setting the bowl down with a thump on the wooden table, she returned to the stove, putting distance between her and the man's provoking scrutiny.

"Ick!" Joanne scrunched up her face. "You want to be licked by a cow?"

"Well, now that you mention it, that's happened a few times already and, *nee*, it's not what I'd prefer. I'd rather have a kiss from a four-year-old *maedel*." To the little girl's shrieking delight, he swept her up in his arms and presented his bruised cheek. Giggling, Joanne shook her head wildly. When Aaron expressed comedic dismay, she reached out a petite hand and gently laid it on the reddened skin.

Returning to the table with the roast, Miriam watched, dumbstruck, as Aaron closed his eyes in blissful contentment at the action.

"Ahh. That's just what it needed to make it feel better." He opened his eyes to smile at the little girl. "How did you know?"

Miriam focused on her path to the table, weaving between the remaining Zook children. Quietly releasing a long exhale, she was glad Aaron's attention was on the little girl he was carefully setting on her feet and not on the more foolish older one who had been stunned to distraction at his genuine smile.

When everyone settled into their seats, she was glad to find that hers wasn't beside the disturbing hired man. Albeit sitting across from him wasn't much of an improvement.

They all bowed their heads. Miriam silently thanked the Lord for the meal and the opportunity to work. While waiting for Isaiah Zook, as head of the household, to signal prayer time was over, she couldn't help adding an appeal to *Gott* to find the man across the table another job. Preferably one on the other side of the district. Grimacing at the unworthy request, she had no time to examine why she'd made it before Isaiah cleared his throat, announcing it was time to eat.

The first thing she saw when she lifted her gaze was the dancing blue one of the man across from her. Shoulders stiff under his unwanted regard, Miriam resolutely picked up the bowl of potatoes and dished out portions for Joanne and two-year-old Abram, who sat on either side of her. Hopefully, the Zooks abided by the adage "every time a sheep bleats, it loses a mouthful," and the meal would be silent.

It wasn't.

"I'm glad to be able to attend church this Sunday," Esther spoke from where she sat with the *boppeli* at the end of the table. "Although I don't know that little Uri here and I will be able to stay through social time."

Isaiah glanced over to his wife and youngest son. "I'll take you home after the service."

His announcement was greeted by quickly stifled groans from ten-year-old Magdalene and eight-year-old Philip, the two oldest Zook children. Miriam suppressed a smile. She remembered when she was young and enjoyed Sunday afternoons that were as exuberant in play as Sunday mornings were in solemnity.

"I can stay with the children. If it's too far to walk home, I'll ask my *bruder* Gideon to take us home later in the day." Miriam knew her offer was appreciated when, below the surface of the table, Joanne grasped her hand and gave it a quick squeeze.

Although Miriam knew the children would enjoy time to socialize, the offer wasn't all for them. Having been in the district for only a few months and busy during that time, she was glad of opportunities to gather with the community. She sat with the unmarried women as was customary at church, but most of the folks she'd become acquainted with so far were couples, friends of her married *breider* and the Masts. She wouldn't be staying in Wisconsin; after Levi's letter, she'd soon have her own marriage to think about back home. But while she was here, it'd be pleasant to get to know more of the unmarried folks her age in the Miller's Creek area.

"Miriam needs to get out and meet more in the community. Particularly if we're going to convince her to stay."

Miriam blinked in surprise when Esther punctuated her comment by sending a smile in her direction. Surely she hadn't spoken her thoughts aloud?

Before Miriam could respond, Esther turned

her attention to the new hired man. "Aaron, I don't know if you've been attending the Sunday night singings lately. But would you mind attending the one tomorrow and bringing Miriam home afterward?"

Miriam's knife screeched across the plate, propelling the piece of roast she was cutting for Abram off it and on to the table. Her ears felt so hot, she nearly dropped her cutlery in order to tug the edges of her *kapp* and cover the fiery tips of them. Instead, feeling the weight of more than a few stares, she hastily retrieved the meat and carefully set it on Abram's plate where she cut it into tiny pieces as her mind whirled.

Socializing Sunday after church, *ja*, but she hadn't planned on staying for the evening's singing. Taking a girl home after Sunday night singing was indicative of expressing your interest in her. With Levi back in Ohio, Miriam wasn't going to be interested in any fellow in Miller's Creek. Even if she was, the last man she wanted connected with her was Aaron Raber. Wanting to throw her hands up and shriek *"ach, nee!"* at the suggestion, she instead tightened her fingers around the silverware and straightened in her chair. Exhaling deeply to regain control of her skittering heart rate, she forced a smile. "*Denki*, but that isn't necessary—"

Her demure rejection was drowned out by a decisive voice from across the table. "*Ja*, I'll do it."

Miriam shot a glare in his direction, only to have it tangle with the challenge in Aaron's mocking eyes. Knowing she'd have no success heading off the disastrous situation from that direction, she shifted her smile to one of entreaty and turned toward her employer. She was met with a canny smile on Esther's face as the older woman looked between her and the irritating Aaron. With dismay, Miriam wondered if she'd misheard that it was Rachel's *mamm*, Susannah Weaver, who was considered the district's matchmaker, and not the woman at the end of the table. Whatever her motive, Miriam didn't want to upset her employer so early into her new job.

Her shoulders sagged. It looked like, whether she wanted it or not, she had a ride home from the singing tomorrow night.

Aaron hadn't been to a singing since before he'd left for the *Englisch* about a year ago. Since he'd been back, he hadn't been tempted, knowing it would feel strange when all his previous Sunday night singings had culminated in taking Rachel Mast home. But he hadn't been able to resist accepting Esther's request when he knew how much doing so would irritate the woman sitting across from him.

He'd done some thinking since their interaction this afternoon. He could continue to wallow in his frustration with the way things had been since he'd returned to the district, or he could do something about it. Aaron decided as he was milking cows in Isaiah's congenial company that he was finished wallowing. If he was going to be accepted by the community, he needed to increase his efforts to get there. What better target to practice on than her, presumably the toughest nut to crack? It was more than obvious she didn't like him. Besides, he'd had too little joy lately to be able to resist the temptation to poke a stick at a growling wildcat.

As far as the singing? Stifling a grimace, he stabbed a piece of roast. *Ach*, he wasn't getting any younger. And he did want to marry someday. A primary way of courting in the Amish community was through attending singing. But after years with Rachel, Aaron had no clue as to whom he might consider courting now.

Although a large share of the rest of the

district was reserved with him, that hesitation hadn't spilled over to the *youngies*, particularly the unmarried women. Having had his ego bruised upon his return, Aaron was glad of their enthusiastic reception. Still, it made him realize how much being connected to Rachel all those years had shielded him from other women's attention. Had he wanted to be sheltered? He wasn't sure. Though appreciative of and comfortable with women, he was a firm believer in one at a time. During the months he'd been away, although there'd been ample opportunities, he hadn't dated any *Englisch* women. It hadn't seemed right when, even though he knew his feelings had changed, he'd considered himself connected with Rachel. Aaron's lips twisted as he thought of his sister-in-law. And he still was, just not in the way he'd envisioned.

Forking another piece of roast, his gaze dropped to the hands of the woman across the table. Aaron frowned as he considered them. It wasn't the clenched fist, revealing Miriam's opinion of the recent discussion, that disturbed him. It was the red, chapped appearance of both slender hands. He winced. Due to his carelessness, he'd contributed to their state by making her redo the laundry.

Aaron's frown deepened. The Zooks had a

washing machine. He noticed anything with a motor. But although he'd listened for it—those motors were very noisy—and glanced from the barn in that direction more than a few times, the machine hadn't been put into use. The manufacturer didn't make them anymore, having long ago transitioned to electric ones. But the simple sturdy motors still worked. Did she not know how to use it? There was one way to find out.

"I noticed the gas washing machine," he commented casually as he helped himself to more potatoes. "Amazing how those are almost a hundred years old and still functional."

The women shared a look and frowned. Isaiah grimaced and shook his head. "*Ach*, not currently functional. I can tell when my cows feel off almost before they can, but with something mechanical? *Nee*. I need to take it in but haven't had the time lately." When his wife pinned him with a stare, he amended, "Haven't *made* the time recently."

"I've had an interest in motors for a while now. I'll take a look at it for you sometime."

Isaiah reddened slightly at his wife's continued attention. "For sure and certain, that would be appreciated."

Aaron's smile was mild considering the excitement he felt. This opportunity to show his skill as a mechanic would be a strong step in the direction of starting his business. He couldn't help but notice Miriam's considering gaze on him. All the better. Sunday would be an opportunity to make amends for what happened this morning. Although the look on her face advised he'd better aim for just attempting to make amends. Actually making them with her might be beyond even his talents.

Hopefully attending the singing would put him on the way of making amends with the rest of the district. Thankfully he and Ben were on good terms now. And Rachel? Aaron cocked his head. Rachel seemed truly happy with his *bruder*. Besides, she had such a sweet nature that she'd easily forgive anyone. Not like the woman across the table.

Aaron poured gravy over the potatoes and his second helping of roast. Even in the dim gas lighting, the evening seemed brighter. Maybe it wasn't the lighting. Maybe the glow was finally starting within him again. Must be why he hadn't looked forward this much to a Sunday night singing—and the ride home afterward—for a long while.

# Chapter Three

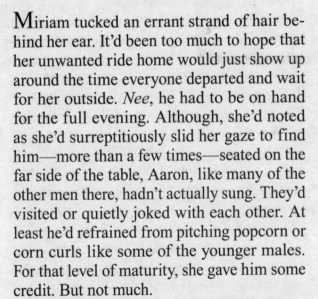

Miriam tucked an errant strand of hair behind her ear. It'd been too much to hope that her unwanted ride home would just show up around the time everyone departed and wait for her outside. *Nee*, he had to be on hand for the full evening. Although, she'd noted as she'd surreptitiously slid her gaze to find him—more than a few times—seated on the far side of the table, Aaron, like many of the other men there, hadn't actually sung. They'd visited or quietly joked with each other. At least he'd refrained from pitching popcorn or corn curls like some of the younger males. For that level of maturity, she gave him some credit. But not much.

Standing with a knot of young women after the farewell song had been sung, Miriam had to admit that even with his presence, the singing, her first in Wisconsin, had been a fun evening. In Ohio, Levi had attended the events only infrequently before she'd left— too much frivolity and the purpose was no longer necessary, as they'd seemed headed for an understanding anyway. But Miriam had enjoyed dressing in identical colors to her "buddy bunch," calling out favorite songs, speculating over who might ride home with whom and pumping friends for information about their older brothers.

Her lips curved at the memory. She'd been queried for enough information about Malachi, Samuel and Gideon over the years to fill up an edition of the weekly newspaper, *The Budget*, that many Plain folk subscribed to. There'd been a multitude of sighs from single women when her three *breider* moved to Wisconsin, where Malachi and Samuel had since married. To her surprise, Gideon wasn't here tonight. No telling where he was or what he was up to. Or if he was already seeing someone. Amish courtships were usually kept under wraps until the wedding was announced in church. Miriam had no doubt she wouldn't find out about a relationship of Gideon's until then. For as much as he teased her, he was remarkably agile in avoiding any topic directed toward himself.

"What's he like at home?"

Lost in reminiscing, Miriam blinked, uncertain if the question had been directed at her. She turned to see the giggling girl standing by Sarah Raber. Miriam stifled a snort. No point wondering who *he* was. The speaker's eyes were directed toward Aaron. Sarah's older *bruder* wore a casual smile on his handsome face as he talked with a group of young men on the other side of the room. Aaron—the man who, regrettably, was Miriam's ride home for the evening.

Assessing the avid gazes of all the other women, Miriam lifted a hand to her mouth to cover her scowl. Aaron's departure would be watched like a hawk. She didn't want everyone to know they were leaving together. If Aaron couldn't be subtle in leaving—and he didn't appear to have a subtle bone in his body—it would be up to her to sneak out and wait for him somehow. A heavy sigh escaped through her fingers. While she very much liked her new employer, she wished Esther hadn't put her in this position.

"Aaron?" Sarah's brows rose. "I really don't see him much. He's either working somewhere or out tinkering in the shed with some kind of motor. He's always been more interested in them than horses."

"Does he still have the car he had when he was with the *Englisch*?"

A shiver ran down Miriam's back. Aaron had a car? Why should she be surprised? In the larger collection of Amish districts where she was from in Ohio, several young men had cars during their *rumspringa*. She hadn't seen much evidence of that here in Wisconsin in a smaller, more conservative district, which she'd been relieved about. But then, other than church, she hadn't been around the *youngies* that much.

"*Nee*. He sold it shortly after he returned." Sarah laughed. "Watching it go down the road, he looked like he was losing his best friend. But it wasn't long before he bought the fastest horse Samuel Schrock could find for him."

Miriam suppressed a smile. Her *bruder* was the local horse trader. He bred horses and bought some locally, but obtained much of his stock from the harness racing track. If anyone could find a fast horse, it was Samuel. Waspishly, she hoped the one he found for Aaron Raber gave the man trouble.

"I'd rather he had a slow horse." Miriam glanced in unison with the others to a simpering young woman. "If ever I got into a buggy with him, I'd want the ride to last for as long as possible."

Mid-eye roll, Miriam realized Sarah Raber was watching her. Abruptly, she schooled her expression to somber attentiveness. She liked Sarah, whom she'd met when the young woman had come over to Rachel and Ben's to see the infant twins, her niece and nephew. Miriam didn't want to offend someone she was hoping would become a friend. She didn't want to offend anyone, except perhaps the subject of the tittering conversation. Sourly observing Aaron as he laughed at something someone in his group had said, Miriam wondered how a sweet girl like Sarah could be related to her older *bruder.*

"It seems strange, now that he's back, to not have him paired up with Rachel. I mean, I know courtships are supposed to be kept secret, but everyone knew they were together. They had been, ever since Rachel and I started our *rumspringa* together when we turned sixteen."

Miriam opened her mouth to retort that her previous employer had made a much better bargain in marrying Benjamin Raber instead. But with Sarah's attention still on her, she thought better of it, closing her mouth with a click of teeth.

She needn't have bothered. Someone said it for her.

"*Ach*, he left for so long and no one knew if he was coming back. Besides, I saw her with her family the other day. She looked perfectly happy."

"Married to Ben? Who wouldn't be?" quipped one of the gathering. During the chorus of giggles, Miriam snuck a glance at Sarah, wondering what the girl thought of the discussion regarding her brother. When the brunette caught her gaze, Sarah rolled her own eyes before putting a hand over her mouth, obviously hiding a smile. The ploy didn't work, as the girl's laughing eyes revealed her amusement. Miriam turned away with her own grin. Although she'd tolerated similar conversations about her own brothers back in Ohio, as much as she'd missed them, in that regard, it'd almost been a relief when they'd moved away.

To her dismay, the first person she locked eyes with was the topic of the conversation behind her. Miriam's smile froze momentarily at Aaron's raised eyebrow. Her grin thawed at the same pace that his smile grew. He was looking at her with the same laughing eyes as his sister. Only his didn't invite her to share the joke. Miriam spun back to face the group.

They… She wasn't sure what they did, only

knew they unsettled her tremendously. What rattled her completely was sensing his approach behind her. She wanted to wiggle her way into the crowd to escape him, much like a spooked steer would. It was hard telling what the unpredictable man would do. The last thing she wanted was his focus on her among a group she was hoping to develop as friends.

Thankfully, he had the attention span of a mayfly. In the time it took to cross the linoleum of the large kitchen, he'd apparently forgotten about her. His gaze had shifted to other, more approachable countenances, and there were plenty of them. The gathering of women parted upon his approach, much like the Red Sea must've split before Moses. In a moment, Aaron was at the center, the rest of them clustered around him like petals of a daisy. Upon finding herself swept up in the middle, Miriam quickly worked herself to the outer perimeter. But not before the rapidly converging group briefly pressed her against his side.

Absently rubbing her arm where it'd made surprisingly heated contact, Miriam gazed wryly at the backs of pleated *kapps*. Tilting her head, she studied the taller dark-haired man they surrounded. Aaron must've had his hair cut very short while living with the *Englisch*. Even with some months' growth since he'd returned, it still hadn't grown out long enough to resemble the bowl-cut style the rest of the men wore. Maybe that was his intent. Maybe he wanted to stay more *Englisch* than Plain. Miriam frowned. All the more reason to avoid him.

"Are you cold?"

"What?" Miriam shifted her attention from one Raber to find another standing at her elbow.

Sarah nodded to the arm Miriam continued to rub. "Are you cold?"

Miriam hastily dropped her hand. "*Ach, nee*. Just…thinking," she finished awkwardly.

Sarah gave an exaggerated shiver as she looked out the nearby window to the snow-covered yard. "I'm thinking I'm glad our district isn't like some of the Swiss Amish communities, where buggies, courting or no, are still required to be open."

Miriam nodded in agreement. "I'd heard one of the reasons they finally allowed closed courting carriages was because *Englisch* kids would hassle courting couples by jumping on the backs of passing buggies. But I think it's more likely they realized it was foolish to ride out in the open during winter."

"Especially up here in Wisconsin." At a burst of nearby laughter, Sarah's lips twitched as she considered her brother. "Rachel told me that when Aaron started giving her rides home after singings in the winter, he had no blankets in his buggy so she'd have to sit closer to him to stay warm."

Miriam's eyes rounded in indignation. "That's… That's…" Her gaze swiveled to the man grinning at a bevy of women a few feet away. That's exactly what she'd expect of him. Seemingly feeling her attention on him, Aaron's gaze joined hers. He winked. Miriam's eyes narrowed into a glare.

Folding her arms over her chest as heat crept up her neck, she turned back to Sarah. "I don't suppose you happen to have an extra blanket available?"

Sarah's own eyes rounded. "Don't tell me you and Aaron…"

"Not by my choice." Honesty compelled her to continue. "Or his. Esther Zook asked if he would bring me home, as she wanted me to be able to attend the singing." At least that's what she'd said was the reason. Miriam kept silent about her suspicion that the woman was attempting to play matchmaker. She didn't need a matchmaker, something she needed to remember when Aaron's amused eyes unsettled her. "Besides I... I have a beau at home."

"I'll sneak a blanket over to Aaron's buggy and leave it if he doesn't have one already there."

Even though she knew it'd take subzero temperatures with gusting winds before she'd do any cuddling with the man, Miriam impulsively grabbed Sarah's hand and gave it a thankful squeeze. Following a smile and nod of farewell, Miriam located the evening's hostess and offered her help in cleaning up from the singing. She refused to appear to be loitering while Aaron attended to his admirers.

She almost jumped when, broom in hand, she closed the closet door to find him beside her a short while later.

"Ready to go?"

"I think the question should be, are you?" Her voice was as frosty as the weather outside. To Miriam's dismay, a quick glance over his shoulder revealed several sets of eyes watching their conversation. Faces revealed the obvious hope that the conversation wasn't what the watchers were assuming, that there was still a chance Aaron might offer them a ride home.

Miriam snorted. Sure and certain, as the

Amish set great store on marriage and family, it was most, if not all, young Plain women's aspiration. But couldn't they aspire a little higher than Aaron Raber? Certainly he was good-looking, with his teasing blue eyes and dark hair. And his way of looking at you—as he was now, as if you were the only one in the room, in the whole county. Maybe the whole state. But there were many more important things to consider when choosing your special someone. Work ethic, for one. Responsibility, for another, which the man before her didn't seem to know the definition of. Although, Miriam had to admit, he was here to take her home as he said he would.

"I've been ready for the past twenty minutes."

"Sure didn't look like it. I'm surprised you're able to tear yourself away." Miriam flushed guiltily at her acerbic words. This wasn't the way her *mamm* had raised her. "I'm ready whenever you are," she added more quietly. "But I'd...rather not go out the door together. I'm only doing this because I couldn't figure a way out when Esther suggested it."

To her surprise, Aaron nodded in understanding. "I'll help carry out the benches to the church wagon. Once they're loaded, I'll just stay outside. Work for you?" At her nod, he moved to join the farmer whose home had been the location for the church service that morning and, as was customary for the logistics of moving benches and hymnals, the evening's singing as well.

Moments later, Miriam frowned as she snuck a look at Aaron's broad back exiting the door. He may not want to be seen leaving with her any more than she wanted to be seen going with him, but at least he was being decent about it.

She kept her broom in brisk motion. Finishing the sweeping and a few other tasks for the appreciative hostess, she determined that surely the fifteen minutes he'd been outside would be enough. Grabbing her cloak and bonnet, Miriam slipped out the door. The cold night immediately enveloped her hands as her gaze swept the yard to pick out Aaron's rig from the collection of similar-looking buggies—at least on the outside—that dotted the yard.

It'd been a wonderful evening so far. Aaron had behaved better around her than she'd expected. But she wished the Zooks lived closer so the ride home would be short. And hopefully Samuel had indeed sold Aaron a very fast horse.

\* \* \*

Aaron straightened from his relaxed slouch against the upholstered seat of his buggy the moment Miriam stepped out the door. When she'd descended the steps of the porch, he slid the buggy's door open to reach out a hand for a subtle wave. He smiled at the obvious sigh that lifted her shoulders under her cloak. Good thing he'd reasserted his sense of self, at least where women were concerned. Otherwise her obvious reluctance would've stung instead of challenged him.

The cold, clear night air carried the rumble of car motors. Aaron tensed. Normally he enjoyed anything engine related. But these weren't the sounds of *Englischers* driving home from an outing on a Sunday night. What made these throaty growls wouldn't be found under the hoods of vehicles on a normal car lot. He'd instantly recognized them.

And knew why they were prowling around an Amish neighborhood.

He glanced again to where Miriam was picking her way across the rutted icy farmyard to his buggy. His foot now tapping on the buggy's floor, Aaron slid his hands down the winter-cooled fabric of his pants to wipe the sweat from his palms. *Slow down, Miriam. Don't get near me before they arrive.*

His hooded gaze cut to the trio of lights that topped a small hill a distance down the country road. Creeping closer, their rumbling engines were now loud enough to draw the attention of the horses in the farmyard. They, as well as the young folks outside, turned their heads in that direction. Darting a look back to Miriam, he saw, to his relief, she'd stopped to talk to another black-cloaked woman.

The growl of the engines grew as the cars neared the edge of the small pasture where many of the buggies had parked for the day. A beam of light burst from the second vehicle to sweep over the rigs, pausing to linger on any people it found. Aaron hissed in a breath. They had a spotlight. Miriam and the woman beside her lifted their hands to block the bright beam from their faces. Dreading it, expecting it, Aaron resolutely faced the road. He refused to cringe or cover his own face when the light landed, and settled, on him.

They'd found him.

He wasn't surprised. With a heavy sigh, Aaron flexed his hands. A few soft pops emitted from them as he pulled on his fingers. At least it'd taken them this long once they'd heard he was back. He thought he'd recognized one of the boys in town earlier this week. He'd ducked back into the hardware shop, hoping he hadn't been recognized himself. Too late. So now that they'd found him, what were they going to do about it?

Whatever it was, it apparently wasn't going to be right now. After a few sinister moments of dwelling on him, the beam blinked off in seeming satisfaction. With a low rumble, the cars crept past the end of the lane. The rumbles erupted into roars when the first, immediately followed by the others, catapulted down the road, causing some of the horses to shy and others to whinny in distress.

Expression grim, Aaron's gaze followed the cars until they were out of sight. His heart rate hadn't yet returned to normal when a scrape on the buggy step outside advised him his passenger had arrived. Distracted, he frowned when he realized it was coming from his right door. Sliding the door open, he found Miriam standing on the step next to him.

The face surrounded by the black bonnet was pale. "I'm not sitting on your left, the side a wife would sit on. I don't want anyone to get the impression we're courting."

Given what his future might now be, Aaron couldn't imagine anyone wanting to court him. Or be associated with him. It was probably safer for them that way. Glancing toward where the lights were finally absorbed by the night sky, he rubbed a hand over his jaw. "Um, listen, if you want to ride home with someone else, I can certainly understand it." He looked past her to the few remaining buggies in the yard. "I can flag someone down if you want me to."

Her jaw dropped at his offer before snapping shut with such a click of teeth that Aaron winced at the sound.

"I figured you for irresponsible. But even I'm shocked at how right I was. What is it, you found someone else who'll be a much more… amiable companion for you?" Vaporized air billowed into the buggy at her heated words.

Thinking of his previous companions who would now be anything but amiable, Aaron shook his head. "*Nee*, that's not it."

"You can't seem to follow through on even a little task. I worry for Isaiah's cows."

"I take *gut* care of the cows," he retorted. Maybe responsibility hadn't been his strength before, at least not where it should've been, but he'd resolved to do better now. At the continuous clatter of hooves, he looked past where Miriam perched on his buggy step. They were drawing the attention of every buggy that headed down the lane. Pretty soon she'd have no other options. "Do you want me to get you another ride?" he bit out.

"*Nee*. Unlike you, I do what I say I will. I said I would ride home with you, detestable as the notion is, and I will."

"*Ach*, then, get into the buggy."

She stayed rooted to the step. "Not on the left side."

Aaron regarded her with exasperation. She glared right back. Instead of pale, her face was now flushed. With a start, Aaron realized his foot was no longer tapping, nor was tension any longer grabbing at the back of his neck like it wanted to strangle him. The adrenaline surging through him had lost its virulent edge and was now just…invigorating.

Poking a stick at the bobcat seemed just the remedy to more ominous thoughts. His face relaxing into a smile, he nodded to the reins. "You want to drive too?"

"*Nee*. I do not want to drive. I just don't want to sit on the left." At the jingle of a bridle, Miriam glanced toward where his gelding was bobbing his head in impatience. Aaron was surprised the restive animal had stayed still this long. She turned back to him with a smirk. "But if you don't think you can handle your horse, I'd be happy to drive."

"I can handle this rig. Or anything in the nearby vicinity."

To his delight, instead of stammering or blushing, the smirk morphed into a smile. To Aaron, a disconcertingly dazzling one. His still settling heart rate unsettled for an instant. Compressing his lips, he stayed silent, not wanting to be the one who began stammering.

"I would imagine you'd think so. I would imagine you'd be wrong. Probably not the first time in your life, nor the last."

Aaron glanced in the direction where all evidence of the trio of cars had disappeared. She was certainly right on that. He should never have gotten involved with them. Not his first, probably not his last, but definitely his biggest mistake. Although it looked like it would be an uphill struggle in some areas, he was ready to work to get resettled into the community. The churning in his gut at the thought of leaving it again surprised him. Because next time, his departure would have to be permanent.

He turned back to find her worrying her lip as she studied him. Twisting on her perch, she looked back to the one remaining buggy in the yard. "If it really is an issue, I see that Jacob hasn't left yet. He works with my brothers at Schrock Brothers' Furniture and lives in the direction of the Zooks. If I ask, he might give me a ride. I'm sure Esther would understand."

Esther might understand, but for the moment, Aaron didn't want to explore why the notion of Jacob Troyer taking Miriam home bothered him so much. With an exaggerated sigh, he scooted over, shifting the blanket that lay there to his other side as he did so. To his relief, after eyeing the lap quilt for a moment, she slid onto the place he'd just vacated and draped it over her lap.

"Is this your sister's?"

Aaron frowned as he directed the eager horse down the lane. "*Nee*, why would it be?"

Miriam tucked her hands under the cover. "Just asking."

"My *mamm* felt bad when my…um…wedding quilt was given to my *bruder* upon his rather abrupt marriage, so when I got back, she made me a buggy blanket." Aaron turned the gelding onto the country road, the tips of his ears burning with the admission. It wasn't as painful as it had been; still, he was glad when she didn't pursue the topic…exactly.

"Hmm. Sarah said Rachel told her you didn't keep a blanket in your buggy so she'd have to sit closer to you to keep warm."

Aaron furrowed his brow at the allegation before shaking his head with a low laugh.

"Cold weather doesn't generally bother me. I guess I did tell Rachel that. It was cover for the fact that I never remembered to bring a blanket along. At the time, I'd rather she thought I was flirting than forgetful." Now, eyeing the surprisingly enticing girl seated next to him, he didn't feel so much the desire to flirt, but to get to know her better.

"Would you sit closer to a guy to keep warm?" Aaron wanted to see her face, but only a minimal profile was visible under the brim of her black bonnet.

To his delight, she turned toward him, her mouth at a downward slant. "To you? *Nee.* If there were a polar vortex, I'd still take my chances."

"Ah…so there is someone you might sit closer to in order to keep warm."

"Not here."

Aaron ruminated on that. Did she have a beau back in… Where was she from? Ben hadn't mentioned anything about that, although he hadn't asked. It wouldn't be surprising. She was an attractive girl. Although why someone would let a girl out of his sight if he were truly interested… Aaron turned his attention to the snow-filled ditch that fringed the road. The snacks he'd consumed that evening suddenly roiled in his stomach. He'd done just that when he'd left Rachel. Eager to abandon the reminder, he looked over to Miriam when she spoke.

"It's not quite this cold in Ohio. But it's not the cold that would have me scooting over."

Although the gelding was fighting the bit in his desire to race for home, Aaron was in no hurry. He kept the horse at a slower jog. "What would it take to have you scooting over in Wisconsin?"

Her gaze slid toward him even though her posterior did not. "Someone different from you."

A grin spread over Aaron's face at her quip. Based on what he'd heard from the single men at the singing tonight, Miriam would have lots of local options should she be interested. Aware of the many female gazes on him when he'd stepped out the door tonight, he knew there'd been an equal number of male ones watching for Miriam to leave the house. Even though she was beside him only due to his employer's request, Aaron was glad he was taking her home. She was just what he needed to get his mind off Blake and his cohorts. His smile faded as he finally let the gelding spring into a ground-eating trot.

Now that they'd found him, what were they going to do?

\* \* \*

Miriam sucked in a surprised breath when the buggy seat lurched under her as the gelding put on a burst of speed. Samuel had indeed found Aaron a fast horse, which was...too bad. She'd been enjoying herself more than she wanted to admit. Although for sure and certain she'd never settle down with a man like Aaron, he was a stimulating adversary.

When the cars had rumbled up, followed by the light striking her face, she'd wondered if her heart was going to pound right out of her chest. The beam had quickly moved on, but only Rebecca Mast's concerned grasp of her elbow had kept her from momentarily sagging to her knees. She wanted to believe she was brave on most things, but when it came to fast cars and bright lights, she was not. She didn't want to embarrass herself by being a blubbery ninny in front of Aaron, but he'd instead been a handy target in which to channel her fear. And her frustration of it. When it seemed that he was going to embarrass her further by passing her off like an old shoe, it'd provoked her even more. Before she knew it, she'd stopped shaking.

Miriam snuck a peek at his clean-cut profile. He might be distracting to spar with. But she still didn't like him.

Aaron stiffened abruptly when the horse jerked up its head. A quick glance at his side mirror was followed by a sharp inhalation. His hands flexed on the reins. Miriam's breath caught as, over the *clip-clop* of the gelding's hooves, she heard the throaty growl of car engines. Twisting on the seat, she looked down the dark blacktop behind them to see a series of headlights piercing the night. Coming fast. Swiveling back, she saw Aaron glance again behind them as well. When he faced forward, his face became as frozen as the passing landscape.

Miriam's eyes widened at the abrupt transition from charming teaser to this iron-jawed forbidding profile. The roar of engines intensified. Breath coming in shallow pants, she looked behind again to see the vehicles had made swift gains on them. The horse was agitated. Its steady cadence had dissolved to an erratic gait as it waffled between nervous prancing and shying toward the ditch.

Miriam eyed the ditch herself. They were at risk of the vehicle coming upon them before the driver could notice the orange triangle indicating a slow-moving vehicle and the *Ordnung*-approved lights. But beyond that, a shiver unrelated to the cold weather ran up her spine at the menacing approach of these vehicles.

She scarcely had time for a shaky exhale before the cars were upon them. Grasping her hands together in her lap in a white-knuckled knot, she dug her short nails into her palms. The frightened neighs of the gelding were obliterated by the roaring engines. The horse reared to such a height it would have fallen over if not for the expert hands on the lines.

The first car zoomed past them. Miriam bit off a shriek when instead of whizzing on, the red glow of brake lights flashed and the car swerved to pull in front of the fractious horse. A screech reverberated in the cold night. The second car, instead of passing as well, braked to keep the now creeping pace of the fretful horse. Miriam didn't have to look back again. She could tell by the illumination surrounding them that the final car was within inches of the rig's back wheels. They were trapped.

The passenger window of the car pacing them rolled down. A young man, a ball cap turned backward over dark hair, leaned out the window. Miriam flinched when he tossed a crumpled aluminum can at the buggy's door. It banged against the window before clattering on to the blacktop. Her frightened gaze fastened on Aaron. Although his focus remained riveted on the skittish horse before him, his jaw knotted. Another can hit the window. With a mutter, Aaron reached over to slide the buggy door open.

"It's about time, Raber. I was afraid we were going to have to do something drastic to get your attention." The man paused, his head cocked as he tried to peer beyond Aaron into the buggy. Miriam shrank against the back of her seat, subconsciously tugging the blanket up to the dangling ribbons of her *kapp*.

"I heard you been back for a while. And you hadn't even looked us up yet. That just makes me feel bad. You left without saying goodbye all those months ago. Where'd you go? Did you miss us?" The man cackled at his own joke.

Aaron continued to stare ahead, his attention on the horse, his hands easy, his expression anything but. "Like a dog misses the ticks he's finally able to shed."

The man spread his hands as if in shocked dismay. "Well, that ain't very friendly. Because we sure missed you. We missed you so much that we look forward to making up a lot of time with you. Don't we, boys?"

"That isn't going to happen." Aaron's tone was as flat as the road ahead. "Because I'm done with you."

"I can't tell you how sorry it makes me to hear that. I'm just plain heartbroken. Plain, get it?" The man laughed again. Miriam had never before regarded the sound of laughter as ominous, but this man's laugh affected her like fingernails on a chalkboard.

"I'll just have to think of a way to persuade you to reconsider, Raber." The car engine revved. The buggy jolted when the horse lunged ahead at the sound. Miriam gasped and braced a hand against the dash as she slid across the seat.

Their harasser leaned farther out of his window. "Now who's in there with you, Raber?"

There was a pause, followed by a bright light being shined into the buggy. Flinching against the blinding glow, Miriam turned her face away.

"Well what have we here? Have you got a girl in there with you, Raber? She's not that brunette I saw you around with before. Hey boys! Raber's tastes must be changing, because this is one pretty blonde. Hey, Blondie! You don't want to stay with this guy. Why don't you come 'jump the fence' with us? That's the term isn't it, for leaving the Amish for us *Englisch*?"

Leaning back, Miriam withdrew her hand from the dash, her moves as careful as if she were confronting a rabid animal. Flattening herself against the seat back, she wished she dared scramble over it into the dark recesses of the buggy. The rumble of the cars' engines vibrated in her chest, battling with the frantic beat of her heart. Pressing her clasped hands into her lap, she squeezed the captured fingers so tightly her bones ached. At the touch of a cold hand, she hissed in a fractured breath.

# Chapter Four

She was trembling. Unable to otherwise vent his frustration under Blake's watchful gaze, Aaron gnawed the inside of his cheek.

He had to get her out of here.

Their joined hands blocked by his body, Aaron kept his stony glare on the smirking face of the man whom, years ago, he'd been foolish enough to get involved with. Despite his resounding tension, the squeeze he gave the frigid fingers in his grasp was gentle. When the slender digits slowly flexed under the contact, he reluctantly let go. Shifting his hand to the reins, his fingers twitched on the leather. Flinging up its head, the horse jolted to a fretful stop. Brakes squealed from the trailing vehicle. Aaron flinched, bracing for a crash. The jarring bump set the gelding to rearing again. It took all his skill and attention to maneuver the horse to a shaking stand. The car beside them rolled past at the buggy's abrupt halt. White taillights joined those that glowed a sinister red as it backed up to again be parallel to the buggy.

Aaron gritted his teeth. Both his passenger and his horse quivered under the ensnaring cars' barrage of thundering engines and bright lights. Fumes from idling engines wafted into the buggy, an odor Aaron used to relish. Now he closed his throat against the stifling stench. He longed to glance over to see how Miriam was doing. He dared not, knowing Blake watched him like a hawk watches cornered prey.

He forced a negligent smile onto his tension-frozen face. "You're wasting your time, Blake. She don't mean anything to me. I'm just giving her a ride home as a favor to someone else."

Miriam twitched beside him. *Ach, nee!* Aaron willed the woman beside him to keep quiet. *Miriam, I know you have spirit, but this isn't the time to reveal it. Not to these people. They'll just want to break it.*

"Tell him he'd do me a favor if he let me give her a ride home."

Hands already curled into tight fists, the rest of Aaron's body stiffened as well at the suggestive hoot from the unseen driver of the car. If he were alone, he knew what he'd do. Knew what he was tempted to do at least, even though it was against the district's *Ordnung*. He'd use his clenched fists to defend the woman beside him. But with several men surrounding them and Miriam vulnerable should he fail, such an action would be foolish, even if the rules of their faith and district didn't forbid it.

Rejecting the option, he searched for others. He had a fast horse. He knew the back roads and fields well. But he also knew the power of the engines rumbling beside him. He should. He'd worked on all three of them, fine-tuning the vehicles to their throaty roars, increasing their horsepower one forged piston at a time. Although it might damage their precious cars, he wouldn't put it past Blake to order that the buggy be rammed. The insidious *Englisch* man kept a stable of vehicles, and surely he'd found more fools like Aaron to work for him.

And if he wasn't successful in getting away, the last thing Aaron wanted was to be in the same situation in a more remote area.

He'd have to find another way.

Sweeping his tongue over a dry upper lip, he searched for a solution. It came to him with a twist in his stomach. *Lie. Or at least stretch the truth.* He'd done it well enough before he'd left. To himself, to others. It was something Aaron had hoped to leave behind. But why not? The best lies were sprinkled with truth. The determination was bitter on his tongue. Blake was certainly no stranger to deceit. Now, if only he'd buy it from someone else.

Mollifying his glare, Aaron lifted a shoulder, hoping the action didn't look as stiff as it felt. "What would you expect, Blake? I'm just finding my way back into the community. I guess I'm glad to hear at least someone is happy to see me. Because the rest of the district doesn't seem to be."

"Ah, come on now, Raber. Are you telling me they didn't go out and kill the fatted calf for you? I'm disappointed."

Attempting a swallow against his Saharan throat, Aaron camouflaged his failure with a derisive grunt. "My family was glad of my return. As for the others? They're a little more suspicious. I need some more time to regain the credibility I lost when I left before I work with you again. Folks are watching. I don't think you'd want anyone asking questions or following me."

He hooked an insolent thumb in Miriam's direction. "As for her? I accepted doing the favor tonight because of her looks. Didn't take me a quarter of a mile to realize it was a mistake. And I'm thinking it'd be a mistake to say too much with her here as well." He touched his fingers to his thumb in a rapid repeating motion, imitating a mouth opening and closing. "Women." He shook his head. "Not the time or place for a serious discussion."

Blake's eyes were hooded as he peered into the buggy. Aaron took up as much space of the buggy's opening as possible. His whole body vibrated in his purposeful sprawl.

The *Englisch* man frowned. "Well you just hurry up on that then, Raber. And while you're at it, don't think I won't be watching you. You take too much time," the man's lips curled in a sinister smile, "and I'll give you a little reminder." With an abrupt pat on the side of the car, Blake ducked his head back into its interior. Under Aaron's grim regard, the window rolled up. Sensing the restive rocking of the buggy, he tightened his grip on the lines. The gelding reared as, with a roar, the car beside them squealed its tires and shot away. The one behind them zipped past as well, blasting a wave of auto fumes through the open door into the buggy. Peeling out, the car directly before them followed in roaring pursuit.

Aaron didn't release his breath until the three sets of red taillights disappeared from his view. When he fractionally loosened his grip on the reins, the gelding, needing no further urging, lurched into a brisk trot. Aaron slid the door shut with a rattle, the only sound other than the rapid *clip-clop* of the horse's hooves on the blacktop. Shifting a hand from the lines, he fisted it at his side. From the moment he'd seen one of his old cohorts in town, he'd been watchful, edgy as to when they'd track him down. He'd been expecting this confrontation. But he hadn't expected it to involve anyone else. He glanced in Miriam's direction.

She hadn't moved. Hadn't spoken.

"Are you all right?" Eying her pale face, Aaron didn't know why he'd asked. It was obvious she wasn't. A bead of sweat trickled down his back. Was she going to cry? He grew pale himself at the thought. His younger sisters probably would bawl, given the situation—even Sarah, the least meek of them. And they'd be justified. He'd seen bold men quake in confrontations with Blake and his crew.

Aaron braced himself for the sight and sound of tears. How was he going to handle a sobbing woman and a fractious horse at the same time? Watching her strained features, his conscience gave a sharp tug. She was an innocent victim in an ordeal of his creation. Regardless of what the horse did, he'd deal with it later. With a hard swallow, Aaron tucked the reins between clamped knees, freeing his arms to comfort a weeping woman.

"Does it look like I'm all right?" In the quiet confines of the buggy, the muttered words weren't a question.

Aaron dropped his arms to his sides. Another time, he might've responded to her sarcasm. But ill with the knowledge he'd put her in this awful position, he dipped his chin to his chest. "*Nee*. I'm..." What was he, beyond a fool to have ever gotten involved in the gang in the first place? Aaron didn't have an answer as a myriad of emotions boiled inside him—anger, self-disgust, wariness, unease for the future. But there *was* one thing above all that he truly was.

"I'm sorry."

Under the black bow securing her bonnet, her slender throat bobbed in a swallow. The lips he'd figured would be trembling in conjunction with streaming tears were as firm as the concrete floor in the Zooks' milking parlor.

"Apparently you're acquainted with these people." Again, it wasn't a question. She turned to face him with a gimlet stare. Her nostrils flared with rapid breaths.

Aaron drew back, blinking in confusion. He'd been expecting to soothe a frightened kitten he'd protected from a trio of vicious dogs, only to have the creature instead snarl and hiss at him. If it hadn't been a pacifist Amish kitten, she'd have probably swatted him with needle-like claws. Although she was still trembling, it was obvious he wasn't going to be comforting a weeping woman. Frowning at the tinge of regret that rippled through him at the knowledge, Aaron reclaimed the reins from where he'd secured them between his knees.

"*Ja.* Before I left I used to...work with them." It was a painful admission, and the first time he'd made it to any Amish person. To any person at all, for that matter. He didn't know why he was making it to her, whom he barely knew. His gaze dropped to her hands, clenched on the blanket's edge in white-knuckled fists. The moments of uncertainty, frightening even for him before the taillights of the three cars had disappeared into the night, washed over him. *Ja*, he knew why. She deserved the truth.

And maybe it would be as the bishop and ministers said—that confession would be *gut* for the soul. His lips twisted wryly. His soul certainly needed it.

He faced the road ahead. "I was a fool."

She snorted. "At least I know now that you're going to speak the truth."

Aaron scowled. "I suppose you never did anything foolish in the early years of your *rumspringa*?" He turned in time to witness remnants of a flinch cross her face.

So she had a few regrets as well. Aaron supposed he was small-minded, for he felt better that the oh-so-disapproving woman had made a few poor choices in her past. Although he couldn't imagine they'd been as wretched as his. He faced forward again. They weren't the first Amish youth to stretch the limits in their run-around years. They wouldn't be the last. But hopefully the hapless decisions other *youngies* made wouldn't choke their future the way his were putting the squeeze on him.

"I was a fool for cars. For trucks. For lawn mowers and ATVs. Anything that had an engine. I studied all I could about them. Worked on whatever I could get my hands on. Got a legitimate job working on small motors and then one working on cars for a while. When

I met Blake, and he found out about my…obsession, he said he had a better job for me."

"An illegal one."

Aaron bit his tongue to stifle his retort. He didn't mind being small-minded if she was going to be so high and mighty. Counting the *clip-clops* of the gelding's eager pace, he reminded himself this whole situation was his fault. And she hadn't asked him to tell his tale. He'd chosen to do so.

"For a while, he was right. I couldn't believe how fortunate I was. It was a dream job. Working with cars. All sorts of cars. Doing things I never imagined. And I was being paid well for it. I was *gut* at it. Too *gut*."

"So you kept working for him."

His breath shuddered out on a self-derisive sigh. "I discovered it wasn't such a dream job after all. And *ja*, I was an imbecile." Hunching a shoulder, he glanced over to find her lips pursed and eyebrows raised.

"I didn't say it."

"*Nee*, but you certainly thought it."

"Someday you'll learn to stop assuming you know what I'm thinking."

He grunted. "I don't have to assume. Your thoughts are written on your face plainer than the words in the *Ausbund*. And unlike the

German in the songbooks, they're easily interpreted in any language."

Her lips twitched. It almost looked like she was suppressing a smile, but surely that was one thing he was misinterpreting.

"*Ja*, I learned it was far from legal. By then, I'd also discovered it was a job a lot easier to obtain than it was to leave." He looked away, fixing his gaze on the large white barn of an Amish homestead they were passing instead of on her disapproving face. "And since I couldn't easily leave the job... I left the community. It wasn't an easy choice. But it seemed the best one for many reasons at the time. Some more of which you know about." He rubbed a hand across the back of his neck at the memory of how he'd hurt Rachel with his abrupt departure. "I'm not proud of any of it."

"*Gut* thing, as humility is a cherished value in our culture."

Eyes narrowed, he shot a glance in her direction at the prim comment. This time, her profile was as smooth as the moonlit, pristine snow-covered fields they passed.

"Are you going to tell the Zooks? Or anyone else?"

She frowned. "You did this before I knew you." Her tone advised that she wouldn't mind not knowing him now. "It's not my business." She faced him with lowered brows. "But if there's any possibility those men will bother the Zook children…"

Aaron felt hollow at the possibility. "I will make sure that never happens." He didn't know how, but he would. Surely even Blake wouldn't go that far…

"All right then." She dipped her head in decisive acknowledgment. "At least as far as I'm concerned, your future with the Zooks or anyone else in the community will not be affected by your past."

He scowled at her emphasis on the last word. "Thanks. But I better watch myself in the present, huh." How had he ever considered comforting this woman?

"Again, you said it. I didn't."

Slumping against the seat back, Aaron directed his attention to the road ahead. He'd said enough. And regrettably, he *had* done enough in his past to make his present a little shaky—if he wanted to stay in the community. Gazing at a countryside that looked like an *Englischers'* greeting card with its well-kept farms tranquil in the moonlight, his chest tightened under the lined corduroy jacket. He wanted to stay. He'd missed his home in his self-imposed exile. His thoughts skimmed over the past few days working at the Zooks', attending the singing tonight with his friends, reconnecting with others as he tried to find his place in the district.

But whether he joined them or not, what he wanted here could be poisoned by Blake and his crew, now that they'd found him.

He swallowed bleakly. At least suffering the tart comments of the irritating woman beside him was better than dealing with her sobs. He'd rather take the sourness she'd displayed than see her frightened and defeated, the way she'd looked when the cars had roared around them. Aaron almost wished the gelding, settled now that the horse knew he was on the way to the barn, would give him more trouble. At least that would be a distraction from his disquieting thoughts.

Miriam spied the silhouette of the Zooks' farmstead in the distance with relief. Now that Aaron seemed absorbed with his own thoughts, she closed her eyes and quietly panted to dissipate the tension that still thrummed through her system.

It'd been a desperate struggle to keep from dissolving into tears. The lights. The noise. The chaos. Her worst memories had cascaded upon her. She'd tasted the fear and shame of that long-ago night. When the cars had disappeared, for a moment it looked like Aaron was going to offer solace. She couldn't let him. If he'd offered comfort, she'd have succumbed to it and assaulted the passing neighborhood with her weeping and wailing. The only way she'd held herself together was by channeling all the overwhelming emotion into anger and boldness instead of frightened sobs. She grimaced. He probably—and rightfully—thought she was a shrew. She slid a narrowed glance at her companion. Although Aaron was frowning, he seemed to have survived her barrage.

Miriam surreptitiously studied him. He'd told her some of his past, and accepted the responsibility for it. She respected that. But she couldn't respect that he'd done something illegal.

Her experience with *youngies* in *rumspringa* was from Ohio. Although she'd heard the smaller, more rural communities were a little more restrained, she knew youth, no matter where, could get pretty wild during their run-around years. Several stretched or ignored the *Ordnung*, but even though they broke the rules of the community during those years, Miriam couldn't condone breaking all laws. Against the outer chill, her cheeks burned at the memory of her own experience.

The behavior and suggestive comments of the *Englischers* had been disturbing, but her primary terror was the reminder of the situations from her past. For reasons she didn't want to examine, instead of being irritated that he'd involved her in his troubles, Aaron's presence beside her had given her a sense of security.

Her lips twisted. Well, she'd unsettled his sense of security. She wouldn't tell on him, though—not unless the children were in danger—as long as his nefarious business affected him alone and no one else. Besides, she owed him for not tattling about the snowball. She couldn't be a telltale when he wasn't. But those men seemed dangerous. For his sake and anyone potentially touched by those menacing characters, she hoped Aaron worked his way out of whatever he'd been involved in. Legally.

As they approached the Zooks' lane, the horse flicked his ears, apparently confused as to why they would be slowing down to turn in to where his master worked during the day instead of continuing on to the Rabers' place where Aaron headed in the evenings. When he wasn't doing a favor for his boss's wife, that was.

Biting her lip, Miriam braced a hand on the dash to prevent being jostled against her silent companion as the horse reluctantly swung into the lane. The man beside her was much more than she'd figured him to be. Much more trouble, that was.

# Chapter Five

Miriam refused to blink first. Her adversary was a worthy one. In silence, they stared at each other. Finally, her opponent broke. With a throaty growl punctuated by a few warning clucks, the hen dared Miriam to disturb her off the nest. Having played this game out for the past few days, Miriam knew the chicken's peck was as fierce as her cluck. Her hands sported a few blue bruises since her first introduction to the Rhode Island Red two days ago, the morning after the singing when little Delilah admitted she was afraid of the creature. Miriam had volunteered to trade jobs with the six-year-old, tangling with the bad-tempered hen in exchange for Delilah doing a quick daily sweep of the kitchen floor. The arrangement seemed to be suiting all parties, except for the chicken. If the Rhode Island

Red weren't such a good layer, Miriam would be tempted to suggest her for the next batch of chicken and noodles.

In absence of that preferred outcome, she'd come up with a method to outsmart the bird. Maneuvering her tool, Miriam carefully slid a small handleless shovel in front and under the bird, feeling absurd gratification at every *ping* when the hen struck the metal in front of her with its vicious beak. With the chicken safely distracted, Miriam slipped her other hand into the nest to retrieve the eggs.

Withdrawing the shovel, she smirked at the glaring chicken. "Ha! Gotcha again." Easily gathering the rest of the eggs in the henhouse, she set aside her handy tool. Ducking out the door, she left the dimly lit warmer coop for the brisk sunny morning. Across the farmyard, the Zook children, from the twins on up, were filing out of the house to leave for school. Unsurprisingly, Philip detoured by way of the barn, trailed by six-year-old David.

It hadn't taken the boys long to become attached to the new hired man—the coworker she'd barely spoken to in the past few days, much to the obvious curiosity of both their employers. Sliding the egg basket's handle to the crook of her elbow, Miriam folded her arms across her chest and watched as Aaron, apparently just finished with milking, stepped through the barn door to greet the two boys. She had to admit, although the man apparently wasn't *gut* at following the laws, he was surprisingly *gut* with the children.

With a frown, she flicked a piece of straw off one of the eggs. He'd been surprisingly *gut* at other things as well. Including the sense of responsibility she'd scoffed at as beyond his ability. Arriving early. Leaving late. Aaron had done all but stay the night at the Zooks' farm the past few days. All while being surprisingly circumspect to her. He must've taken her comments from Sunday night seriously indeed.

Maybe just as seriously as she'd been thinking about those remarks herself. Remarks she'd blurted out after the distressing situation. Comments that displayed an attitude of which she was ashamed. The past few evenings, after blowing out the lantern on her bedside stand, she'd stared at the ceiling, shifting uncomfortably at the memory of her sanctimonious words.

It was wrong to break the law. Laws of the *Ordnung* and laws of the country. But self-righteousness was also something their faith frowned upon. The *Biewel* stated to first cast the beam out of your own eye before calling out a brother about the speck in his. Although Aaron's past may hold more of a branch than a speck, Miriam knew as she continually tried to put distance between herself and her biggest regret that she was guilty of figuratively donning bifocals in order to see the dirt in someone else's eye.

Other Bible verses, memorized long ago, marched through her mind then and every time she caught Aaron's wary gaze on her. Verses about all having sinned and coming short of the glory of *Gott*. About judging not, lest ye be judged. Miriam gnawed on her lower lip. She was guilty of them all. She wouldn't say anything about the questionable decisions of Aaron's past. But she certainly shouldn't even be thinking of judging him when her own impetuosity had taken her to jail. And then there was their faith's strong belief in forgiveness.

"*Denki* for taking care of Rhoda."

The childish voice at her elbow had Miriam blinking a few seconds before she remembered Rhoda was the bad-tempered hen. She smiled at the girl currently counting the eggs by pointing at the eye-level basket with her finger. "It's no problem, Delilah."

"She scares me."

"She scares me, too," Miriam confided.

"But sometimes, if I try really hard, I figure out a way around my fear."

Delilah made a face. "Do I have to too?"

Miriam bent to straighten the black bow of the girl's bonnet. "When you're ready. In the meantime, I'm glad you took over sweeping the floors. That was always my least favorite job."

The girl's blue eyes rounded at the admission. "But it's easy."

"Maybe for you." Miriam tapped a gentle finger on the girl's nose. "Maybe it's because you're closer to the floor."

Delilah giggled. "You're tall, but you aren't *that* tall."

Both gasped when a snowball whizzed by to splatter over Miriam's shoulder with a *thwack*. Having grown up with three older *breider*, Miriam moved instinctively. Not knowing whether further assaults were coming, she swept the little girl behind her as she searched for their attacker.

Responsible Magdalene, already halfway down the lane, swiveled toward them, her mouth agape. The boys, the likely culprits, were still at the barn. Philip and Aaron wore bland expressions as they faced each other in apparent deep discussion. Miriam narrowed her eyes at the pair before dropping her gaze to David. Delilah's twin was striving to keep a straight face, but he couldn't suppress his huge grin and the eyes that kept darting in her direction. Philip's lips began twitching as well when he reached out to swat his little brother on the shoulder. At the boys' feet sat two lunch pails amid the fresh snow from the previous evening. Snow that was pristine except for footprints. And divots big enough to dig out a few snowballs.

Miriam immediately set down the egg basket to scoop up a handful of snow herself and hurl it at the trio. Her missile smacked Aaron on the top of his head, knocking off the stocking cap perched on the crown of his dark hair in apparent concession to the warmth of a milking parlor crowded with cows. She herded a giggling Delilah toward cover at the side of the chicken coop. Magdalene dashed to join them. Miriam fired a few more snowballs to cover her flight.

The boys scattered to find their own refuge. David ducked through the barn door. Abandoning his cap, Aaron vaulted with Philip over the board fence into the cow lot. Miriam could see their hands reaching under the bottom board to scoop up ammunition from the undisturbed snow. With David currently shut out of the action in the barn, she and the girls were able to force the other two to keep their heads down. Their efforts hit with *thunks* on the white-painted boards, not doing much more than showering the guys with spattered snowballs.

Miriam's fingers were red with icy remnants of snowballs caught between them when the barn door opened and a figure stepped out. Apparently expecting to see her little *bruder* emerge, Magdalene gasped with dismay when she hit her *daed* square in the chest. The farmyard went from a flurry of activity and excited shrieks to absolute silence.

With a deadpan countenance, Isaiah brushed the white residue from his jacket. "*Gut* shot. You must've been enjoying a lot of baseball at recess. Next time we play at home, we'll have to have you pitching. But speaking of recess, am I mistaken, or isn't this a school day?"

A chorus of exclamations and groans accompanied the Zook children as they hastily appeared from their shelters and snatched up their abandoned lunch pails to gather around their father. Chagrined at her role in the impromptu battle, Miriam followed at a slower pace, snagging the egg basket on her way across the yard.

Aaron lithely vaulted the fence. Miriam

frowned as he approached their employer from the opposite direction. Either Aaron or one of the boys with him was the culprit in throwing the first snowball. Was he going to accept responsibility, or redirect it? It would be a way of getting her in trouble after her threat. Even though she deserved it. But she wouldn't have fired back if not fired upon first.

Spying his stocking cap on the snow, Miriam snatched it up. Impulsively, she slipped one of the eggs from her basket into the *woolie*'s opening. She'd never tell on him, but if he told on her, he'd discover she wasn't beyond a little retaliation. Reaching Isaiah and the children, she held the hat in a loose grasp from the arm that supported the egg basket in its crook. Already regretting her spontaneous action, she waited for a moment to subtly retrieve the egg.

"We'll have to run now," bemoaned Magdalene, brushing the last few bits of snow off her *daed*.

"I can't keep up when we run." Delilah's lower lip quivered.

"It was my fault." Miriam's gaze snapped over at the strong male voice. Aaron was wiping snow from his hands. His dark hair was dusted with icy crystals. The sight of it gleaming in the early morning sun arrested her attention, or maybe it was his strong profile as he accepted responsibility, whether or not it was his to accept. Despite the chill of her hands and feet, a flush of heat surged through Miriam as she gawked at him. Her eyes narrowed. She hadn't ever thought so before, but maybe Aaron was as handsome as her previous employer, his younger *bruder*, Ben.

The *woolie* hat was plucked from her nerveless fingers. Miriam instantly grasped for it, but David was already handing it to Aaron. His gaze still on his boss, Aaron absently took it, holding it by one side of the rolled top. All eyes but Miriam's were directed at Isaiah. Hers were pinned on the gray hat dangling from Aaron's capable tanned fingers.

"*Ach*, I've been in a snowball fight or two. And as I said, I'm impressed with the skill of my *kinner*. We'll have to play more baseball this summer. But since we have snow on the ground now, how about a game of Fox and Goose after milking tonight?" He smiled as the apprehensive faces of his surrounding children transitioned to ones of excitement. "And in the meantime, if you'll help load the milk cans in the wagon while we get the team hitched up, maybe Aaron will give you a ride to school before he drops the milk off at the cheese factory. I imagine the milk can handle it today if Samson and Prince trotted on the journey."

With squeals of approval, the children moved in a herd toward the wagon where they quickly stowed their lunch pails before disappearing into the door to the milk house.

*"Denki."* Aaron grinned at the older man.

With an open mouth and a futile outstretched hand, Miriam watched as Aaron spread the hat's opening with both hands and swung it up to pull it down over his hair. When his blue eyes widened, she squeaked and slapped her hand over her mouth. Isaiah's jaw dropped when yellow yolk flecked with bits of brown shell dribbled down Aaron's lean cheek.

"Maybe I better hitch up the team while you, uh, get ready to go."

Aaron's gaze narrowed on Miriam, whose own eyes were rounded. Her lips rolled in so much she felt the stretch of skin under her nostrils.

Isaiah eyed her expression before his gaze dropped to the egg basket on her arm. He rubbed a hand over a mouth that obviously fought a smile before scratching his beard. "When you, ah, take the eggs into the house, Miriam, I think Esther was wanting to talk with you about going to the bakery. She was putting a list together. Might as well combine the trips with the one into school, as Aaron will be heading in that direction anyway."

"Oh, I'd be happy to stay home with Abram and Uri if she wanted to go instead."

At Miriam's hasty response, Isaiah rubbed his hand over his mouth again. "I imagine you would. But she said she felt she had enough of an outing the other day at church." He glanced toward the wagon where the children had worked out a process to move the heavy milk cans. "Looks like if I don't hurry, the *kinner* will have the wagon loaded before I can get the team harnessed." With a final nod at Aaron, Isaiah gave a cough that sounded suspiciously like a snicker. "Um, you might want to get that cleaned up before it dries or freezes." Having issued the advice, he turned and strode toward the barn.

And left a wary Miriam to face an expressionless Aaron. She cringed when he fingered the goo on the side of his cheek, bracing for his deserved ire to rain down upon her. The mess on his face had been unintentional for sure and certain—*ach*, if maybe not the intention, at least the actual occurrence—but she'd gone too far.

He opened his mouth. She held her breath.

"Looks like the...yolk's on me." Aaron's

face was impassive but the blue eyes that held hers danced.

Miriam snorted. Then she snickered. When the corner of his mouth farthest from the mess lifted in a smile while the sticky side remained rigid, she burst out laughing. Pressing her hand against her stomach, she doubled over with mirth when he tugged off the stocking cap to reveal more yolk, egg white and eggshell. Straightening with effort, Miriam lifted the edge of her apron to stem the tears of hilarity that streamed from her eyes.

Following a long inhalation through her nose, she held it a moment before releasing it slowly through pursed lips. "I didn't mean to do it." He raised an eyebrow, the one not encrusted in yellow. She started giggling again. "Well, I did, initially. But not after you took responsibility for the fight. I'm so sorry. Here, let me help."

Reaching up with the apron, she dabbed at the side of his face. With the cold, the mess had begun to congeal. Her efforts only managed to smear it further. Miriam trapped her lower lip in her teeth. "I'm so sorry," she repeated, meeting his droll gaze. Her brisk movements slowed as her fingers absorbed the firm lines of his cheek and jaw beneath the thin cotton of her apron. When he encircled her wrist in a warm palm, she froze, her breath trapped in her throat.

"I'd been thinking about our discussion the other night." This time the smile expanded to both sides of Aaron's face. At the action, flecks of congealed egg yolk smeared by her apron dropped onto the shoulder of his jacket. Miriam's gaze followed the falling debris as, with curious relief, she broke eye contact.

"I'm certainly not without sin," he continued, "so no stone-casting for me. But I didn't think the *Biewel* said anything about a snowball. And if I remember correctly, I owed you one. Now it seems I owe you an egg as well."

His grasp, though gentle, was unyielding. Miriam didn't resist when he lowered her hand to her side. "I promise," she vowed, "any egg that I…serve you in the future will be fried, scrambled or poached." When he slowly opened his fingers, releasing her, she used her now free hand to snag the soiled cap from his loose grip. "And I will wash this for you."

He gave a startled laugh. A delightful ripple washed over Miriam at the sound.

"More dirty laundry between us. At least it won't be as big of a load this time." His smile expanded into a grin. "Can we call us even now?"

They might now be even, but Miriam felt

incredibly unbalanced by his allure. She took a step back. Sliding a hand down her apron, she retreated another step. She'd need to change the soiled garment before she went to the bakery.

Miriam was relieved she could remember, after gawking at his gorgeous face, what the errand was, much less that she had one. When she went into the house to get Esther's list for the bakery, she needed to collect a catalog of prudence for herself. Otherwise, she was as foolish as the girls from Sunday night singing. If she didn't watch it, she'd be pestering Sarah for information on her *bruder* like all the other single *maedel*. Except she *wasn't* single; she had a beau back home.

She had a beau back home. The reminder jolted her. She had no business giggling like a fool with another handsome man. Levi was her beau, a fairly handsome one. But comparing him and Aaron was like calling Silver Lake and Lake Michigan both lakes. They were. But there was no comparison between the two.

Of course, it wasn't all about being handsome. It was about character. Strength of character, like Levi had. He'd never get involved in something illegal. Not like the man before her. The thought of her pious beau breaking the law, any law, almost made her snort. She was counting on Levi's restraint to balance against her own impulsiveness. That she needed the balance was as obvious as... the goo on Aaron's handsome face.

Something else she immediately needed was to distance herself—if not physically, then at least emotionally—from the enticing man before her. Sobering with effort when her mouth still ached from her earlier hilarity, Miriam marshaled her defenses, grasping at any straw to push his oh-too-charming self away.

"I don't know. Your comments that night about women, and me in particular, were rather obnoxious."

Aaron furrowed his brow. He didn't need to ask what night she was referring to. There was only one "that night" for them. What happened to the captivating woman who was there a moment before? "I was trying to save you from what I figured was an even more obnoxious situation."

"By insulting me? Some rescue." Pivoting, she marched toward the house, the egg basket swinging in rhythm with every indignant stride of her long legs.

His stocking hat dangled from her fingers. A chunk of shell dropped from it as he watched. Grimacing, Aaron reached up to pick at the egg caking on his skin. *Ach*, she was a snippy one. Once again, he'd expected a purring kitten only to get the hisses instead. She was like a spirited Standardbred filly that'd show you her heels after allowing you to approach, foolishly thinking you'd be able to comb your fingers through her hair… Aaron blinked. *Mane*, he meant *mane*.

Abruptly he steered his thoughts away from the sleek blond hair that disappeared under Miriam's *kapp*. Those heels, if you weren't careful, would kick you straight in the ribs.

# Chapter Six

At the crunch of footsteps in the snow and muted *clanks* behind him, Aaron turned to see Isaiah approaching with Philip driving the team of Percherons behind him. The other three Zook children were in the bed of the wagon along with the collection of milk cans. Isaiah carried a bundle of leather that Aaron recognized as harness breeching and traces.

"Since the harness shop is right by the bakery, if you'd stop there, it would save me a later trip. Tell Reuben these pieces either need to be repaired or replaced. Hopefully not the latter. I'll put them in the wagon while you wash up." The older man's lips quirked above his beard. "Unless you're planning on going as you are?"

Aaron gave his employer a wry smile. "*Nee.* I'll be back in a minute." Before turning toward the outdoor hydrant, he shot a dark look toward the house and muttered, "Probably faster than she'll return."

The hydrant's icy cold water was what he needed to dampen his aggravation with his contrary coworker. To his disgruntled surprise, she was scrambling into the wagon with a fresh apron under her coat by the time he returned.

When Aaron climbed in, he arched an eyebrow at how much room was left on the narrow wooden seat. If his companion scooted over even a fraction of an inch, she'd tip off it. Her going boots-over-nose back into the snow was something he almost wouldn't mind witnessing. But even as provoking as she was, Aaron didn't want to see her hurt. Too bad the Zook children were so well-mannered that they'd left the seat for those who were *supposed* to be adults. He'd rather have sat beside Magdalene, Philip or the twins. He got that Miriam didn't like him—at least at the moment, he amended, recalling those tantalizing shared moments of mirth—but did she have to be so conspicuous about it? Was he supposed to sit so far on his side now that it'd look like a hay wagon could be driven between the two of them?

"We're going to be late."

At Magdalene's quiet lament from behind him, Aaron plopped down in the middle of the bench. Gathering the reins, his lips quirked as Miriam wiggled beside him in her attempt to scooch farther over in the limited space he'd left her. If she wanted to make the trip hanging half out of the wagon in order to keep sufficient space between them, that was her problem. If he made that objective a little bit difficult, well, she was surely up to the challenge.

With a grin, Aaron prodded the huge geldings into action. They lunged forward, the wagon jolting behind them. Tittering on her perch, Miriam gasped. Aaron's smile grew smug when she inched a little closer to him as he urged the geldings into a trot. The children cheered at the increased pace. When they swung out of the lane, Miriam grabbed his arm to keep from lurching off the wagon. Upon realizing what she was clutching, she flung it away. With a grimace, she hooked her arm over the back of the seat for stability.

"Gotcha," Aaron murmured into the brisk breeze.

At the country school, the children scrambled down from the wagon as a young woman was reaching for the rope to ring the bell mounted on the building.

"Just in the nick of time!" She smiled and waved.

With a side-eye to his seat companion, Aaron waved back enthusiastically. It did his ego, bruised by the woman beside him, some good to see the pretty single teacher look back over her shoulder at him with another little wave as she followed the Zook *kinner* into the building. Aaron watched as the door closed behind them.

Grace Kauffman had moved into the area while he was gone. He'd seen her at church after he'd returned. A pretty new girl was hard to miss. A friend had reluctantly admitted Grace's name, apparently not relishing the potential competition. Aaron didn't blame him. If he had a sweet, pretty girl singled out, he'd want to keep her to himself as well. If she was anywhere near as pleasant as she seemed, the young woman wouldn't be teaching more than a year. Women in the district could only teach if they were single. Pretty, congenial Grace would probably be making wedding plans by the time the next school year started.

Unlike the girl beside him. Not if a man had any sense of self-preservation, that was. Pleasant wasn't even in her dictionary.

Keeping the Percherons at a placid walk, he directed the geldings toward the cheese factory. After a silent ride there, he backed the team up to the dock and jumped down to unload the milk cans. To his surprise, Miriam had scrambled into the back of the wagon and was rolling the heavy cans on their bottoms toward the tailgate as he unlatched it.

"There's still a *swish* sound inside so maybe we didn't turn them all into butter on the journey."

Aaron blinked at her smile. Relieving her of the heavy can, he set it on the dock and propped a hand on his hip. "Are you condemning my driving? Too much jolting for you?"

"*Nee.* Not at all. I would've felt terrible if the children were late this morning because of me." She shuffled another can toward the dock. "You did very well getting them to school on time, given the circumstances."

Aaron eyed her warily as they emptied the wagon, wondering when the stinging claws were going to surprise him again. To his relief, they were still sheathed while they made another silent journey to the farm of Reuben Hershberger. Reuben and his sons operated a buggy and harness shop, while his wife ran a small bakery out of the house.

Miriam had climbed down from the wagon and was headed for the bakery before Aaron had the team secured. "Do you need any help?" he called after her.

*"Nee,"* she tossed over her shoulder without hesitating in her stride. "I've got it. Don't worry about me."

Aaron snorted as he collected the harness pieces from the wagon, slung them over his shoulder and turned toward the windowed door that marked the entrance to the shop. Worry wasn't in the vocabulary he'd use in his relationship with the woman. The jargon he relegated to her included *exasperated. Chagrined.* Not to mention *disconcerted.*

And *intrigued.*

*Ach,* he was thinking too much about her. Probably because she was the first single woman, other than his sisters, who didn't get fluttery-eyed when they interacted with him. Even Rachel had been a bit dewy-eyed when they'd first started walking out. Time together had healed her of it, although she'd still regarded him with a sweet smile. Was he a fool to relish an occasional glare? To be challenged by a glowering expression instead of a glowing one?

He touched a hand to his hair, still damp from its recent wetting. Probably.

The scent of leather and harness oil combined with a whiff of wood from the adjacent buggy shop welcomed him when he stepped through the door. Aaron wrinkled his nose at the odor of gasoline that mingled with the other expected smells, its source most likely a generator he could hear rumbling from an unseen location.

Some *Englisch* thought the Amish didn't use electricity. That was far from the case. While district *Ordnungs* might forbid the use of electricity from the power grid—which they believed could open the door to modern devices that might take away their core values—they didn't specifically prohibit the use of electricity. Amish communities generated their own power through a variety of ways: wind turbines, like the windmill he'd noted behind the shop, water wheels and solar panels, which were becoming quite common now in more progressive districts. One of the most common ways for shops and businesses to create electricity was the use of generators, both diesel and gasoline. A business supplying and repairing those and other motors would keep him busy, should he ever be able to start one. Aaron's lips quirked. But for now, he milked cows and shoveled manure.

The door swung shut behind him with a

jangle of bells, leaving him in a room of walls covered with horse collars and harness parts of all kinds. Bins of different-sized horse-shoes, some with traction devices to help handle Wisconsin winter conditions, lined the floor along the edges of the room. Tepid sunlight streamed through the few windows and a couple of dusty skylights.

Aaron set the collection of leather on the counter that bisected a quarter of the room. Leaning an elbow upon the wooden surface, he waited for someone to respond to the bells. After a few minutes, when no one appeared in the doorway that led deeper into the building, he frowned and shifted his position.

"Hello?" he called, hoping his voice would carry over the sound of the generator when the sound of the bells apparently hadn't. A moment later, a youth bumped off the door-frame as he appeared in the opening. As heavy-eyed as the boy looked, Aaron won-dered if he'd awakened him.

Reuben Hershberger had supported the buggy business in the Miller's Creek area for some time. As his boys were getting older, he'd recently expanded the operation to in-clude a harness shop, even sending one son to live with a cousin out of state to apprentice in the craft. Aaron respected Reuben's initiative, but he felt for the man in the timing. Hopefully whatever was learned wouldn't become a lost art. Harnesses were in the midst of moving away from leather to synthetic, using nylon coated in plastic or rubber that protected it against a horse's corrosive sweat. Although more expensive, the material helped the harness last longer with less and easier maintenance. A benefit for every user—even someone diligent in the care of his equipment like Isaiah. Well, diligent at least in everything but the washing machine.

The washing machine. With a wry smile, Aaron glanced out the window to the door where Miriam would've entered the house's lower level, the location of the bakery. He wanted to take a look at the washing machine before Miriam washed his soiled hat. He shook his head. The whole thing really had been funny. Noting her shock when he'd put on the hat. Witnessing her hilarity at the sight he must've made. Miriam had an engaging laugh. It was…refreshing to see a woman who allowed herself to laugh until tears made her blue eyes gleam. The challenge to prompt her to do it again was almost worth the occasional hisses he'd also evoked from her. Almost. As long as he didn't end up with more egg on his face.

Miriam's animation was in stark contrast to the lad who was stumbling to the counter. Reuben's business expansion would be challenged indeed if this was an example of his son's work ethic.

"Are you all right?"

The youth squinted at Aaron as if seeing him through a haze. "*Ja.* What can I do for you?"

*In your condition, probably nothing.* "Is your *daed* around?"

"*Nee, Daed* hired a driver to go to Portage on business. He should be back…soon." The lad squeezed his eyes together. "At least I hope so. The windmill hasn't been working and my *breider* and I had to figure out something else to power the tools."

Now that the boy mentioned it, the windmill wasn't turning, even though a brisk breeze had made it a chilly ride over this morning. That explained the muffled rumble of the generator. Aaron had always figured that hand tools made up the majority of the gear for leatherwork, but hard telling what this farmstead, running at least three businesses, needed for power to support it.

A jangle at the door announced a new arrival. Aaron turned to see Miriam enter the shop.

"I put the bakery goods in the wagon. Are you going to be a while?"

"I don't know. This might take a little longer than I'd anticipated."

"If you're going to be a bit, I'll go back into the bakery and wait where it's warmer." She sniffed. "Where it also smells better, too."

The words were said mildly enough. Aaron didn't know why a dull ache throbbed in his temple at the sound of them. What was it about this woman? He was becoming as contradictory as she was, smiling at the thought of her antics one moment and exasperated into headaches the next.

"What was it you needed?" Grimacing, the boy pressed his hand to his stomach.

Frowning, Aaron gestured to the conspicuous collection of leather on the countertop. "Isaiah Zook would like you...well, someone to repair this if you can. If not, he's interested in replacing it." *And you might want to write that down, because obviously you're not in any shape to assess it now and you also don't seem to be in any condition to remember what I've said the moment I walk out the door.*

*Ach,* he was a fine one to judge. The reminder stung. Folks had probably thought the same about him before he'd left, as his mind and interest had been somewhere it definitely shouldn't have been. Not like the Hershberger family. Aaron's eyes narrowed as he studied the swaying youth. Reuben Hershberger had a *gut* reputation in the district. Prior to Aaron's absence in the community, the whole family was known to be hardworking.

The sound of the motor running in the background suddenly became very ominous. Abruptly, he straightened from his slouch at the counter. "Headache? Nauseous?"

"*Ja*, sorry. I must be coming down with something. What was it you were saying you wanted worked on?"

Darting around the end of the counter, Aaron grabbed the boy by the shoulders and thrust him toward a startled Miriam. The bells clattered wildly as he jerked open the door. "Get him out of here." Hustling to a window, he wrenched it open. "Do you have a cell phone?"

Her hands full with propping up the now sagging lad, Miriam shook her head in obvious bewilderment.

"See if they have a phone shack nearby. Or a phone in the bakery. Call 911. Tell them he has carbon monoxide poisoning. Now get him out of here." Without waiting to see if she followed his directives, Aaron sprinted for the doorway behind the counter. Tracking the rumble of the motor and a heavy-duty cord that snaked along the floor, he sped down a hallway. Just inside an exterior doorway, a portable generator was running. Jostled by the wind, the nearby door was banging against the doorframe. A handle of something—a rake, a shovel—protruded askew between the door and the jamb. With a quick scan of the machine, Aaron located the orange power switch and twisted it.

He sagged against the wall in the now blessed silence. The heavy odor of exhaust made him grimace. Pushing off the wall, he propped the door open with what he discovered was a shovel that lay canted across the opening. Stepping out into a lot dotted with a collection of new and used buggies, he set his hands on his hips and sucked in a few more extended breaths, this time of crisp, clean air.

He should've noted the youth's odd behavior earlier. That was the thing about carbon monoxide. Colorless, odorless, tasteless, it was a silent killer. Aaron touched a finger against his temple. Already his headache was fading. He couldn't imagine how the Hershberger boy felt. He'd been judging the youth and, depending on how long he'd been exposed to the deadly gas, it was amazing the lad could even function. No wonder he'd been confused. Aaron shook his head. *I should've caught it sooner. I would've if I'd been more aware of my surroundings instead of thinking about Miriam.*

Miriam, whom he'd shoved the boy at and left. He needed to check on them. Getting out of the carbon monoxide and into fresh air should help the symptoms, but long-term issues could be created by intensity and length of exposure.

Aaron strode along the back of the shed, his gaze on the motionless windmill behind it. How long had the generator been running inside the shed? The boy had mentioned something about the windmill not working and needing power… Wait a minute! Had he said his *breider*? Aaron jerked to a halt. Were there others somewhere in the shop?

Aaron bolted back into the building. Following the black cord through a doorway, he plunged into a workroom. Two younger teenaged boys slumped over the built-in counters strewn with harness and buggy works. Their heads rested on outstretched arms, their bodies precariously perched on tall stools. Aaron grabbed the smaller one and slung him over his shoulder. Dodging the now silent generator, he hustled through the exit. Once outside, he gently propped the boy against the shed's back wall and raced inside again for the brother.

Hefting the boy over his shoulder, he grunted under the deceptively heavy burden. Like most Amish farm boys, the youth was solid muscle. Although Aaron stumbled under his load, he was glad for the boy's weight, as carbon monoxide affected smaller people and animals more strongly. Would the smaller boy be okay?

Carefully setting the youth next to his brother, Aaron ducked back into the shed. How many *breider* were there? Did he have them all? When a quick scan of all the rooms revealed neither people nor even a cat, he dashed back to the boys. Squatting beside them, he touched a finger to their throats. At the feel of two steady pulses, he sank to the ground with a silent thankful prayer. Hopefully they were only succumbing to drowsiness induced by the monoxide and not unconsciousness.

Getting them into the fresh air was *gut*. But they needed more help and pure oxygen, and they wouldn't get it here. Aaron lifted the smaller lad to his shoulder and lunged to his feet. Rounding the corner of the shed, he was relieved to see the oldest Hershberger boy sitting on the lowered tailgate of the wagon. Miriam stood nearby, her hand patting the youth's knee as she talked on a cell phone.

Aaron carefully laid his *bruder* alongside the older boy.

"Is he going to be all right?" Judging from the youth's increased alertness, some of the effects of the carbon monoxide seemed to be fading. "And where's Enoch?"

"I'll be back with him in a minute," Aaron assured him. "Would he be the only other one in the building?" At the boy's jerky nod, he turned back toward the shop. As he passed Miriam, she reached out to grasp his hand.

"Gabe Bartel is on the way. There's another boy as well?"

Aaron nodded in relief that EMS help was coming. *"Ja."* He couldn't make himself let go of her fingers.

"They're better off in the fresh air, *ja*? As soon as you get back with the other one, I'll run into the bakery and ask for some blankets to keep them from getting cold. I'm sure their *mamm* will want to know what's going on."

"Sounds *gut*. Where'd you get the phone?"

"It's Ezra's." Releasing Aaron's hand, she pointed to the older boy, currently hovering over his brother. When Miriam started talking into the device again, Aaron sprinted back to where he'd left Enoch. As he turned the corner of the building, he saw the boy had both hands pressed to his head. Aaron almost stumbled in his relief that the youth was regaining consciousness. If this one was coming around quickly once he was in fresh air, it increased Aaron's hopes for the youngest Hershberger boy.

Head lolled against the white painted boards, Enoch squinted up at Aaron. "What am I doing out here?"

"Hopefully getting enough oxygen to help clear out your system from the carbon monoxide you inhaled from the generator."

Enoch's eyes widened. "Our *daed* is going to be mad."

Aaron smiled. It was the same response he'd have given at the boy's age. His smile quickly faded. Until he was lured more by what he wanted to do than what he knew was right.

"Where are my *breider*? Are they all right?"

Positioning the boy's arm around his shoulder, Aaron helped Enoch to his feet. "Let's get you to them. I'm sure they'll be glad to see you."

It must've been dust in his eyes that had him blinking at the sight of Ezra assisting the youngest boy to sit up. He couldn't think of another reason for the stinging at the back of them. It couldn't have been anything like the tears that glistened briefly in Miriam's eyes as he reunited the brothers.

The screen door to the bakery entrance banged open. Aaron kept a hand on Enoch to steady him as Mrs. Hershberger ran across the yard, a fist pressed against her mouth. Reaching her sons, she touched them all as if to assure herself they were all right before turning a rattled gaze to Aaron.

"Carbon monoxide from the portable generator," he responded to her unspoken question. Tilting his head to catch the faint sound of a siren, he added, "Help will be here soon." He turned to Miriam. "I think your blanket idea was a *gut* one." With a quick nod, she spoke briefly with Mrs. Hershberger before heading into the house. Ensuring the boys and their *mamm* would be all right for a moment, Aaron trotted to the end of the lane to wave the pickup with its flashing dash light in. The driver's window was already down when the truck came to a rocking halt beside him.

"If you don't mind staying put for a moment, there's an ambulance coming as well." Local EMS Gabe Bartel's attention was already on the trio by the wagon as he made the request. At Aaron's prompt agreement, gravel spurted out behind the pickup as Gabe hastened up the lane.

Aaron watched anxiously from the end of the driveway as Gabe worked on the Hershberger boys. In short order, all three were wearing oxygen masks. When he heard the distant wail of sirens and saw the flashing blue-and-red lights down the road, Aaron breathed normally for the first time since he'd realized what'd been affecting Ezra's behavior. Waving the ambulance in, he followed the vehicle up the lane at a subdued walk.

Knowing he wouldn't be much help with the activity in the farmyard now, he circled the shed once more to contribute where he could. By the time the ambulance drove away, he'd made considerable progress on troubleshooting the immobile windmill. Gabe was packing up his gear when Aaron returned to the farmyard.

"Are they going to be all right?"

Gabe turned to him with a smile. "Time will tell on the youngest one, but it's looking pretty good right now. But for your prompt action, it could've easily been a different outcome."

Aaron blew out a slow breath. "I'm just glad I listened to some of the seminars you'd taught the volunteer fire department."

"You going to join the department again? We could sure use you."

Aaron hadn't thought about it. Previously

he'd done it because it just seemed the thing to do. But now the thought of rejoining others in the district in the work of protecting the community sounded very tempting. And oddly comforting.

"*Ja*. I'll be there."

The ambulance had already been crowded with the three boys. Gabe waited until Mrs. Hershberger addressed what she needed to in her home and home business so she could join him in the truck. Aaron and Miriam waved from the wagon as the two followed her sons to the hospital.

Although she was silent, Aaron felt Miriam's attention on him as they made their own way down the lane at a much slower pace. What was she thinking? Usually he could tell, or at least guess, but there were few clues to her current pensive expression.

Barely a quarter mile down the road, he grimaced.

"What?"

"*Ach*, I left Isaiah's harness on the counter. I hope they figure out who it belongs to."

"Do you want to go back and get it?"

"*Nee*. Isaiah's probably wondering why we're taking so long as it is. I can check on it when I return to finish fixing their windmill."

Miriam cocked her head. "How did you

know what it was? I just assumed he was sick like he mentioned."

"Flu and carbon monoxide poisoning have some similar symptoms. But I was starting to get a headache, too." He gave her a sideways glance, complete with a smile. "One I figured you were giving me."

She winced, then nodded. "That's fair."

Aaron's smile stretched into a grin. Her candidness was refreshing to him. It wasn't the norm for Amish to compliment one another, as doing so might make someone *hochmut*, or proud. But complimenting someone came naturally to him. He liked to do it. And, although it wasn't his aim, it usually got results, particularly from young women. But Miriam certainly didn't leave him many openings. What could he say to her? *Hey, that was a nice verbal comeback? Good aim with that snowball? Wish* I'd *thought of putting an egg in* your *hat?*

If he said any of those things, he knew what the results would be. Another snowball. Or egg. Aaron rubbed a hand over his mouth. It'd probably be the same results if he gave her a genuine compliment. And what would that be? *Your hair is like corn silk? Your eyes are as blue as morning glory flowers on a summer day?* He snuck another glance at his passenger. They were. But *nee*, best not to go anywhere near there. That might earn him a snowball or an egg as well. And if the winter sunlight that struck the blond hair visible in front of her *kapp* caused it to gleam, a sight that earned him a surprising flip in his stomach, well, best not to go there either.

There were safer topics to discuss.

"I like engines, remember?" He shrugged a shoulder. "I started taking the generators apart on the farm when I was about eight. Which didn't make my *daed* happy because it took me a few attempts to be able to put them back together at first. Many of the generators for Amish businesses are built-in. Portable generators, while helpful, can also be dangerous. As they're more infrequently used, folks sometimes forget they must always have ample ventilation. They should never be used inside. Not even right next to a door or just outside where the fumes can funnel back into the building. At certain levels, just five minutes of carbon monoxide exposure is enough to be fatal."

Sighing deeply, he shook his head. "I sure hope Gabe's right and they're going to be okay."

"Me too. Gabe said you saved their lives." She gave him a rueful smile. "You told this

Blake person that you needed to regain the community's trust. This should help."

He scowled. "That's not why I did it. Not at all. And if anyone hears about it, it won't be from me."

She'd misjudged him. Because of his handsome looks and charm that seemed to mesmerize other young women, Miriam had tossed him in the same category as Tobias, a dark smudge on her past. She sniffed. More than a smudge—a whole black page.

Her first impression of Aaron, when he'd been raising his voice to her sweet employer, hadn't helped. But she supposed she might be upset too if she'd returned to find her beau married to someone else, someone who'd already had his child. Miriam waited for the surge of indignation at the prospect of that happening when she went home to Levi Peachy. When it didn't appear, she blinked, a bit disturbed by its absence.

Aaron wasn't the same as Tobias. Still, it was hard not to think in black-and-white when she encountered charming, good-looking men. She knew she shouldn't. Her *breider* were good-looking and, when they applied themselves, could be charming too, especially Samuel. But then, they'd never broken the law. She frowned. At least that she knew of.

*For all have sinned and come short of the glory of God.* Her frown deepened when the verse ran through her mind. She'd confessed of her sin. And repented. And still felt the regret and shame. She snuck a look at Aaron, who remained scowling at the broad black backs of the Percherons. He hadn't even confessed and repented yet. He might even continue to do what he knew was wrong. Miriam folded her arms over her chest. Surely that gave her a little room to judge?

*Judge not, that ye be not judged.* She hissed out a breath as the biblical reminder trailed on the tail of the earlier verse. Aaron glanced over with a raised eyebrow. Miriam turned her face toward the ditch. She couldn't say much about the speck in his eye when she had a log in her own. She hunched a defensive shoulder at her annoying conscience. His sin was more than a speck. Hers was surely not a log, she'd just… Miriam slumped in the seat as she realized she was trying to justify that Aaron's breaking of the *Englisch* law was worse than her trying to twist what the *Biewel* said. *For all have sinned.*

Hadn't he indicated he wanted to get away from this gang? Or had she imagined that?

Miriam swallowed. She needed to admit to him that she was no better than he. After the way she'd treated him since his admission—even before, she realized with a grimace—he deserved to know. With a deep sigh she straightened on the seat and turned toward him. Her eyes widened when Aaron's shoulders stiffened and his thigh flexed as he pressed his foot against the wooden boards that lined the floor of the wagon.

Then she heard it as well. A vehicle was roaring up behind them.

# Chapter Seven

Tension swept through Aaron like swirling water from a burst dam. *Not again. Not so soon.* But Blake probably thought it wasn't soon enough. When Aaron's prior boss gave an order, he expected immediate results. If patience was a virtue, it was one of many the man didn't possess. Which meant Aaron's time was running out. Now that Blake knew he'd returned, Aaron had to make a decision on what to do about his involvement with the gang. The thought of going back made his stomach twist. But how to get out? Leave the community again? The prospect made him yet more ill. How could he get out without leaving the community? He was trapped.

The hair at the back of his neck prickled at the rumble of the advancing motor. Once again, Miriam was caught up in his past mistake.

Braced to face what bore down on them, Aaron swiveled. His shoulders sagged under his corduroy coat as he turned back with a relieved exhale. Her eyes wide, Miriam looked behind them as well. Aaron figured the delivery truck driver was still craning his neck in an effort to see around their slow-moving wagon to the road ahead. He guided the team to the side of the blacktopped country road as they climbed the hill. When they reached the top, the van swung out from behind them and gunned down the empty road ahead.

Miriam flinched at the deafening sound as it roared past. Frowning, Aaron tried for a nonchalant comment, only to discover he had to clear his own nerves clogging his throat first.

"You don't like vehicles?"

"Not the fast ones." The dark wool of her jacket lifted as she hunched a shoulder. "I… don't do well with powerful cars. Or bright lights at night."

He darted a glance at her but didn't comment. Grimacing, Miriam slid her hands up and down over the apron that draped her lap.

"There are many Bible verses about how important it is to confess our sins."

Aaron blinked at the zigzag in the conversation. What did Bible verses have to do with fast cars? Or bright lights with confession of sins? Although, in regard to that, he could envision Bishop Weaver blazing a torch at him as the old minister waited for Aaron to recite all the ways he'd stepped, or leaped, over the boundaries.

As far as Miriam changing the subject? At least it was easier than following her shifting mood. He shouldn't be surprised about the topic, though, since the roar of the passing van probably reminded her of the other night and his history of breaking the law. Did she expect to hear about all the times he'd broken the *Ordnung*'s laws as well as the *Englisch* ones? Aaron grunted. If so, they'd need a longer trip than the one they were on.

"You could probably recite them all," he mocked.

She smiled ruefully. "I know them. But I have my own sins to confess."

He raised an eyebrow. "Ha. I'd love to hear how the proper Miriam Schrock sins. I hardly see you put a foot wrong. And believe me, I've been watching."

"I have my faults."

"*Ja?* I'm sure you could list an encyclopedia of mine. Name one of yours."

Miriam dipped her chin. "I'm too impulsive."

"*Nee,*" he drawled. "How could I believe

that? Oh *ja*. I've been on the receiving end of your snowballs and eggs." And assumptions about him, but unfortunately, she wasn't always wrong there.

Her cheeks flushed to a becoming rose. She picked at the cuticle on one of her slender fingers. "When I first entered my *rumspringa*, I made some poor choices."

Aaron snorted. "Don't we all." Although he was bursting with curiosity, he held his tongue. After the only sound for the length of a field they'd passed was the *clip-clop* of the geldings, he sighed, wishing he had the patience of Job and knowing he fell far short.

"You were the one who said a moment ago that confession was important," he prompted.

She slowly inhaled. "The most handsome and charming *youngie* in my district showed interest in me." She shook her head at the memory. "I soaked it up like a garden in a drought. He persuaded me to do something… against my better judgment. That's why I say I'm too impulsive."

Aaron went cold at her words. His hands clenched the reins with what he'd like to do to the one who'd broken her trust. "Your *breider* should've done a better job watching out for you."

She regarded him with an arched brow.

"What kind of job did you do for Sarah when she entered her *rumspringa*?"

"I…" *I was too busy courting Rachel and thinking about cars to pay much mind.* "I left that to Ben to keep an eye on her. He was closer to her age. Besides, he didn't seem to be interested in pursuing any other girls at the time." He grimaced. "Now I know why. He was interested in the girl I was courting."

Miriam's lips twitched. "Well, that all turned out all right. For them at least."

Aaron smiled. "I think so, too. For me as well, I suppose." He hesitated, gnawing briefly on the inside of his cheek. "Since you're here and he's not, it must not've turned out the same for you and your…handsome and charming man?"

"*Nee. Nee,* not at all. But it turned out much better for me than it did for him."

"I'm glad to hear it." And he was, considerably.

"*Ja.* I'm here. And he's in prison."

The Percherons jerked their heads in confusion when Aaron twitched the lines at her words. Automatically soothing the big geldings, he kept his attention on Miriam's bent head. He swallowed past a suddenly dry mouth. That destination could've been— could still be—his future.

"What happened?" he murmured.

Miriam's attention remained on her lap where her fingers were twisting into a knot. "Tobias invited me to a party. Not one in the district, *nee*, that was too tame. This one was farther away and included many others beyond Amish *youngies*." Her face was in profile. Her mouth, the corner he could see, curled downward. "I was so excited. Of course, I didn't tell my folks where I was going. The party was one where I could wear the blue jeans I'd bought at an *Englisch* yard sale. I brought them and other clothes I didn't normally wear along with me when he picked me up that Saturday in his buggy. We left the buggy at the home of a friend of his. After we'd changed into *Englisch* clothes, we got into a car that he kept there. At first I liked the ride. It was…thrilling riding in its front seat with Tobias driving. Like forbidden fruit. But instead of just an apple, it became the whole tree." Pressing her lips together, she lifted her gaze to the ambling Percherons.

"Once we got on the highway, he started driving very fast. My heart was racing as well. It was the first time I'd been to anything except singings, ball games and local frolics. My *breider* never said anything about doing things like that. But I figured they did." She gave him a wry smile. "Maybe not Malachi,

but definitely Samuel. Several of the *youngies* did."

Aaron stifled a cringe at her words. *Ya*,
several did. He'd been one of them. He'd gone
to enough parties to make up for all the ones
his *bruder* Benjamin had never attended. And
then some. *Look where that got me. Not any-
place I want to be.*

"Although they probably wouldn't admit
it, some girls did, too. There's freedom from
many of the normal rules during *rumspringa*.
Usually the Plain girls don't push the edges of
it quite as much as the boys do. Unless they're
persuaded by the boys. Or foolish and impulsive like me."

She dipped her head again. "I was wondering if he was going to kiss me. I was *hoping*
he was going to kiss me. I was giddy with excitement. Anticipation. Guilt. We were laughing. The looks he was giving me as he leaned
closer made me breathless." She glanced at
Aaron. "You probably think I'm fast."

"*Nee.* Not at all." And he didn't. What he
*was* thinking was he'd like to spend a little
time with this Tobias character at the back
of a barn. Alone. Reminding him of the ap-
propriate way to treat women. But how could
he think that when he'd done the same? He'd

stolen more than a few kisses from Rachel when they were walking out.

Shifting uneasily, Aaron tried to loosen the tension gripping his shoulders. Surely that wasn't...jealousy? Surely not. Surely it was just anger, something he was regrettably quite familiar with. But if it was anger, it was a sort he didn't recognize.

"I stopped laughing when blue-and-red flashing lights showed up in the rearview mirror. I thought it was because we were going too fast. Instead of slowing down, Tobias started going faster and faster. It took me a moment to realize he was trying to evade the authorities. He whipped the car onto a country road, and although he kept going, he turned off his lights. It was terrifying. We'd fly over a hill, and the car would be floating for a moment before it would come back to the road with a screech and jerk. I was flung around the inside of the car a few times so I buckled my seat belt and clung to it and the handle by the window. I'd never gone so fast in my life. But the flashing lights were gaining on us. And now there were more of them."

Her fingers gripped the wooden seat with white knuckles, as if she was reliving the chase. Aaron's own heart was racing.

"He tried to make another corner." Miriam

shook her head. "But we were going too fast. Praise *Gott* that it was a shallow ditch instead of a steep one. If it hadn't been, I don't know what would've happened. The seat belt almost strangled me when we slammed to a halt. Tobias jumped out and started to run. The officers caught him. They put cuffs on him. Two deputies put him in the back of a sheriff's car. I was shaking too much to move. Another officer shined a light on me. Asked me questions. Helped me out of the car. The night was lit up with flashing lights. Sirens were wailing. I was so afraid."

She slowly exhaled through pursed lips. "When they searched Tobias's car, they found drugs. Apparently a lot of drugs." Her voice quavered. "I didn't know he was into that."

Careful not to interrupt her, Aaron hissed in a breath. He'd seen that at some parties, too. It was something he'd always steered clear of. His weakness had been his desire to work with anything mechanical. It'd taken him down the wrong road as surely as something he'd consumed, though. Having had that experience with someone she'd trusted—no wonder she couldn't abide those who broke the law.

Reaching over, he covered her hand with his own, wincing, but not surprised to feel it twitch beneath his palm.

* * *

Miriam was shaking. Had she ever willingly told anyone the whole story before? Well, she hadn't actually told Aaron the *whole* story. Yet. But she would. She could get through the harder part with him. At least she hoped so. He was a *gut* listener, better than she'd expected. Much better than Levi, who would interrupt and admonish her regarding her behavior. Releasing her grip on the seat, she tangled her fingers with his. The clasp of his hand was like receiving a lifeline when capsized in rough water. Her shaking slowly subsided.

Being from her district, Levi had known what had happened, of course. The community didn't need telephones when the Amish grapevine worked so quickly. He'd questioned her about it before they'd started walking out. Probably to ensure she'd gotten that well and truly out of her system and wouldn't ever do something like that again. Although sick with shame, she understood she'd deserved his lecture. But with Aaron, it was actually a relief to admit the mortifying tale. She twisted her lips. Maybe confession of sins was *gut* for you after all.

And now she had to finish the worst part of the story. He gave her hand a reassuring squeeze. She took a deep breath. "Tobias had been planning to deliver drugs to people at the party. The authorities knew he was a dealer. They knew there was a party that night. They'd been watching for him."

Taking another breath, Miriam let it out in a shaking sigh. "I had a purse. The first time I'd used one. Something else I bought at an *Englisch* yard sale. I was so proud of it. The police searched it." She licked her lips. "They found drugs in it."

She paused at the audible inhalation from the man beside her. Miriam braced for him to disentangle their hands. Instead, she felt another squeeze. She closed her eyes against the prickling that threatened them. Clearing her ragged throat, she continued. "While I'd been foolishly thinking he was leaning over to kiss me, he'd been slipping the drugs into my purse. He noticed the authorities before I did. I was shocked. And so scared." Despite her efforts, a few tears trickled down her cheek.

Opening her eyes, she stared down into her lap. "I said they weren't mine. But he said they were. That I knew what was going on. Why would he do that?" She shook her head, still not understanding why a man she knew and trusted would intentionally betray her like that. "It was his word against mine. I'd never had my word doubted before. With no way to prove my innocence, I was put in a separate sheriff's car." She pressed her free hand against her mouth at the memory. "The authorities were very courteous. As courteous, I suppose, as they could be in the situation. But I was so afraid. I thought I was going to be sick on the way to the jail."

Reluctantly releasing his hand, she crossed her arms over her chest. Cold that had nothing to do with the current winter morning swept through her. "They took my...picture. And fingerprints with black ink. I was afraid I'd never get the stains off." Miriam pressed her fingertips hard against her sides. "I spent the rest of the night in a jail cell. I'm petrified now of jails. Just the thought of them." She grimaced. "Later the next day, it was determined no charges would be filed. So I was released. I came out and my...*daed* was waiting for me at the jail." Her nose stung with more tears at the memory. "I've never been so ashamed. He didn't say anything. I...don't know if I wanted him to or not at the time. I couldn't look at him the whole way home. Or my *mamm* when I got there."

She sniffed. "I confessed to them. And later to the church. I know they forgave me—

at least I know my parents did." She hung her head. She couldn't say more. No matter what he now thought of her, she was glad she'd told him.

"But you haven't forgiven yourself."

Miriam almost jumped at his quiet words; he'd been so silent up to that point, a silence she'd appreciated. She sat up straighter. "I vowed that I'd never be so impulsive again."

He raised his eyebrows high enough they touched his bangs. Reaching up, he patted his head as if looking for something. Miriam frowned before she realized what he was searching for. His missing hat. The one waiting to be laundered to remove the splattered egg.

To her surprise, her lips twitched toward a smile. "Or at least I try not to be. At least not on the big things."

"So...no more *Englisch* parties."

"Definitely not." She emphatically shook her head.

"No more blue jeans?"

"Stuffed to the back of my drawer. Haven't worn them since."

"Purse?"

"*If* I carry one, it has a zipper and a strap."

"And I suppose you don't trust handsome and charming men anymore?"

She cocked her head in consideration. "I don't know. When I meet one, I'll see." This time she couldn't prevent a smile as she looked up to meet his warm gaze. Something she'd never thought possible when reminded of that horrible night.

And she had Aaron Raber to thank for it. Something else she'd never thought possible.

# Chapter Eight

Miriam, her hands laden with shopping bags, shoved the door of the Bent N' Dent open with her shoulder. Since the trip to the bakery a few days ago, Esther had stayed home with the *boppeli* and left any errand running to Miriam. Little Uri had picked up a cold and was having trouble shaking it at his tender age.

While Miriam shared Esther's concern for the infant, she enjoyed the outings. She'd been to the Bent N' Dent before with Rachel. It was similar to a store at home that provided overstocked products or those with expired dates or damaged packaging for significant savings. She'd picked up some gingersnap cookies for the children. Hopefully they'd enjoy that kind. If not, well, she would.

A smile etched her face as she crossed the discount store's parking lot toward her buggy. And maybe someone else would as well. Had Aaron ever said what his favorite kind of cookie was? Her smile turned wry. If he'd mentioned it during the early part of their acquaintance, she'd have blocked it out, or made anything else but that kind. But now that she was paying attention to him—and she was paying a lot of attention to him lately, maybe too much—she wanted to know.

Miriam's stride faltered. Any amount of attention paid to Aaron was too much when she had a beau back home. A beau she hadn't thought of lately with her mind too full of someone she shouldn't be thinking so much about. Her grip tightened on the bags. But Aaron wasn't the man she'd thought he was at first. *Ach*, she amended, remembering significant unresolved things from Aaron's past—maybe he was.

But he also had some redeeming qualities. Like a beautiful smile. One of several they'd been sharing lately since she'd confided her mortifying story while he'd quietly listened with patience and compassion. Miriam inhaled a lungful of chilly afternoon air. And if hands had lingered when fingers brushed passing the dishes around the table...

The weight of the bags dragged her shoulders down. She had an almost-fiancé back home. The handle of the bags dug into her fingers. Maybe no *almost* about it. She'd left Levi with the impression that when he was ready to wed, she would be, too. And she was. Just maybe not to Levi.

*Oh Miriam, there you go being impulsive again.* How could she fall for someone this fast? Someone she disliked, *detested*, a short time ago? This was why she needed someone steady, plodding even, like Levi. There was no plodding about Aaron; he was excitement and energy and, surprisingly, responsibility and patience. And oh so many things she was just beginning to realize.

Miriam felt the rumble of the loud motors in her chest before she heard them. For a moment, she was as frozen as the ruts that crisscrossed the parking lot. On suddenly shaky legs, she faced the highway. Three cars rolled by the Bent N' Dent's driveway to glide to a growling halt at the nearby intersection. Miriam's mouth went dry when the driver in the middle car looked in her direction and pointed to where she stood. Before she could react, the cars made a noisy U-turn at the intersection and wheeled into the parking lot.

Too terrified the night of the singing, Miriam hadn't noted many details of the cars that surrounded Aaron's buggy. But even with the baseball cap shielding the upper portion of his face, she recognized the passenger of the dark blue one pulling up beside her, more by his ominous presence than his appearance. If the man didn't seem so...venomous—like a coiled snake—he could have been considered handsome. His hair below the borders of the cap was dark, his jawline chiseled. His eyes, even shadowed by the bill, were a sharp green. They raked her from *kapp* to the soles of her black shoes and back up again. A malignant smile revealed white teeth. Miriam backed up a step when the man's window silently glided down. Her retreat was cut off when one of the other cars pulled up behind her.

"Well, well, well. It's Raber's lovely blonde. Out doing a little shopping today? Did you find what you were looking for?"

Hesitantly, Miriam bobbed her chin in acknowledgment.

"Good for you. Glad someone has. 'Cause I haven't yet." His mocking voice took on an edge. "Raber never got back to me. And that makes me unhappy. You tell him that for me, won't you? That I'm unhappy? Very unhappy. And when I'm unhappy, I just have to take it out on someone." Hooking an elbow on the edge of the open window, the man patted the gleaming dark blue door. "Raber was always good at cars. More so at tearing them down, but he also fixed up these beauties. Did you know that?"

Miriam flinched when a couple of the cars revved their engines before the motors returned to a menacing growl.

"Yeah, he's really good at mechanics. But he's not so good at taking orders. Or communicating. What do you think might help him get better at that, hmm? Maybe seeing what happens when he doesn't?"

Miriam chilled as his gaze swept over her again, the intimidating smile never leaving his face. "And since you're here, and he's not, along with telling him I'm unhappy, maybe you could also take back the message that he needs to be better at taking orders?" His fingers idly drummed against the door of the car. "They say actions always speak louder than words. Boys," he raised his voice, "what kind of actions do you think we could show Blondie so Raber knows we're unhappy?"

"I have a few ideas. And I volunteer to carry them out." The taunting offer came from the car behind her.

The bags in one hand slipped from Miriam's fingers to drop with a thud onto the frozen snow-covered gravel of the parking lot. She longed to hear the bang of the store's door, announcing someone coming to her aid. But she'd been the only shopper in the store, and the older woman tending the register had had enough trouble making out the price tags on her purchases that Miriam didn't hold much hope for rescue from that quarter. The roads in all directions were regrettably empty of any kind of traffic.

Without breaking Blake's mocking gaze, she reached her now free hand into one of the bags she still held. Her fingers curled around a weighty can. Despite the pounding of her heart that reverberated to her fingertips, she reluctantly released her grip. Their faith, as Aaron alluded to the first day they'd interacted, taught to not resist evil but to turn the other cheek. Although her fingers twitched against the metal, Miriam slowly pulled her hand from the bag. *Oh Aaron. I wish you were here now.*

Her cloak brushed the back of her legs as something bumped it. Tearing her gaze from the sinister dark-haired man, Miriam whirled to discover the car door behind her was opening. His eyes hot above a menacing grin, the driver pushed the door farther open. Breathing in rapid pants, Miriam braced against the pressure. Any movement backward would bring her within reach of the gang's leader, whose gaze she felt boring into her back. Her throat, choked with fear and the gas fumes from the idling cars surrounding her, began to close.

Under the onslaught of the door, her feet slipped on the lot's icy surface. Dropping the rest of her bags, Miriam shot out an automatic hand to catch herself. She snatched it back when it touched the vehicle before her, its sleek cold surface vibrating from the powerful engine. Elbows pressed to her sides, she tried to make herself as small as possible. Her pulse outpaced the rumbling tempo. Under the covering of her *kapp*, her scalp prickled. Body tensed, she prepared to run, but where? Escape was cut off.

"Hey!"

At the nearby shout she jerked her attention from the intimidating faces surrounding her to beyond the roof of the car. Her knees almost buckled at the sight of Aaron skidding over the slippery parking surface as he raced toward where she was trapped. His vacated buggy, pulling a flat trailer stacked with feed sacks, continued across the parking lot. The horse cast a wary eye in the cars' direction as he headed toward Miriam's buggy and the watching bay there. She hadn't heard the clatter of approaching hoofbeats over the rumbling engines.

"Leave her alone." Aaron bounced off the rear fender of the car behind Miriam and slid to a halt at her side. Bracing one hand against the roof above the smirking dark-haired man, he clenched his other into a fist and drew back. Miriam grabbed hold of his bent elbow with both hands, the soft corduroy of his jacket a balm for her ice-cold hands. His rigid arm vibrated almost as much as the nearby cars.

*"Nee,"* she murmured. Tugging gently on the stiff limb, she pleaded quietly. "Please." Defending herself may or may not have been against their pacifist nature, but if Aaron threw a punch, even though he hadn't yet been baptized into the church and subject to the rules of the *Ordnung*, his standing in the community might suffer. She couldn't risk it.

Tendons stood out in his neck above the collar of his jacket. Her thumbs gently rubbed the ribbed fabric at the back of his arm in an attempt to soothe. "I'm all right."

Cold air whipped down Aaron's windpipe. His lungs worked like a bellows. Partly from his frantic dash, but mainly from the fear coiled like a viper in his stomach at the sight of Miriam trapped between the cars. His pulse pounded in his forehead. Even as condensation burst into the air with his every breath, sweat trickled down his back.

At a nod from Blake, the man behind them

pulled his door shut with a petulant slam. Although still trapped, they were no longer immobilized. Conscious of Miriam's grip on his arm, he forcibly extended his clenched fingers. Removing his hand from the car's roof, he laid it gently over the icy one at his elbow. Blake's gaze followed the movement. He gave a satisfied smirk at the sight.

"About time you showed up, Raber," he drawled. "We were just about to show Blondie here how disappointed we were that we hadn't seen you since the other night."

"She has nothing to do with…our history." The admission that he *had* a history with this gang made him ill.

"Oh, I know that. And I don't care about our history. I'm interested in our future." Blake looked pointedly at Miriam. He ran a hand along his jaw.

"I run a business, Raber. I have business partners and clients who're depending on me. I hate to admit it, but it's not been quite the same since you've been gone. I suppose you could say we miss your good Amish work ethic."

Aaron pushed a swallow past a cotton-dry throat. "I just want to rejoin my community."

Blake's smile was no longer smug. It was pure malice. "I don't care what you want. And you can rejoin your community. As long as you come back to work with us. If fact, you want community? We've got one. You've already joined us. As you already know, we're a lot harder to leave—if you know what I mean—than your little district."

He did know. He wanted to stagger beyond the cars and be sick at the memory. Miriam shifted closer to him. Aaron resisted the urge to put his arm protectively around her, further making her a target. A dark movement beyond the blue roof of the car had him flicking a glance in that direction to assess the new threat. He sucked in a deep breath at what he saw.

Jethro and Susannah Weaver were pulling into the parking lot. Miriam's *bruder*, Samuel Schrock—his head turned in their direction—was slowing as he approached the store's driveway. The new arrivals didn't say anything. They just drove their buggies up beside the cars and quietly watched. Overwhelmed with relief, Aaron squeezed Miriam's fingers. The door to the Bent N' Dent opened. An older woman stood in the doorway, leaning on her cane. Gabe Bartel pulled up to the nearby intersection in his truck. Apparently noticing the unusual activity in the parking lot, he slowly drove down the road toward the driveway, blinker indicating he would be pulling in as well.

When Aaron looked back to Blake, it was obvious the gang's leader wasn't pleased to see the reinforcements.

"This isn't over, Raber." With a last tap on the car's sleek side, Blake withdrew his arm. The window rolled up. He said something to the car's driver and the engine roared. One by one, the cars spun out, the tail end of one swinging close enough to Aaron to bump him. Although his feet slipped, Miriam's solid presence beside him kept him from falling. He watched the cars spurt onto the road and disappear from view. Willing himself to stop shaking, he gave Miriam's hand a final squeeze before letting go to pick up her dropped bags. Opening one, he looked in.

"*Gut* thing they were bent and dented to begin with."

While Miriam took a few of the bags, he wouldn't relinquish them all. "Rather them than you," she murmured. They started toward where the Weavers were parking next to their rigs.

Aaron pulled out a package and shook it. "I don't know if the cookies survived the fall, though."

Gabe pulled up beside them and rolled

down his window. "Aaron, the younger Hershberger boy was doing all right when I checked. They're all going to be fine. Thought you'd like to know."

"I certainly would. *Denki*, Gabe."

"Everything all right here?"

Aaron bit the inside of his cheek. He couldn't explain what was going on without exposing a part of his history, a part he was too embarrassed to share with this man he'd grown to admire. "Eventually."

Gabe didn't seem satisfied with the response, but he let it go when Jethro and Susannah approached, along with Samuel. Another trio from the community whom Aaron respected. He shifted uneasily under their curious, yet compassionate gazes. To his relief, Jethro recognized his discomfort.

"I hope you d-didn't b-buy out all the cookies, Miriam. Otherwise we m-might starve at our house."

It felt good to smile at Jethro's jest regarding his wife's reputation for poor baking skills.

"I left a few on the shelf." Miriam's rigid shoulders relaxed as well. "But you'll have to beat my *bruder* into the store to get them."

"*Ach*, tempting as it is, the cookies are safe from me. I've come by for potato chips. And peanut butter. And if we didn't have a few shelves of them in the basement, I'd be in for pickles as well. We can't seem to keep enough in the house with Gail…" Samuel paused, and to Aaron's surprise, his face reddened more than the cold weather might generate. Miriam's brother rubbed a hand across his mouth.

Aaron's smile expanded at the sight of one on Miriam's pale face. He didn't know if it'd been accidental or intentional that Samuel had almost mentioned that his wife was with child, a topic usually not discussed in an Amish community. He was just glad that the slip helped Miriam to relax after her frightening experience.

"Anyway, the cookies are safe from me today," Samuel finished in a mumble.

And he and Miriam were safe for another day as well, thanks to this quiet, supportive community. Aaron swallowed against a tight throat. It was one of the many reasons he'd come back. One of the many why he didn't want to leave.

His gaze flicked to where the cars had disappeared. He just hoped he wouldn't have to.

# Chapter Nine

❧

Miriam lifted her head from the pillow. *Ja*, there it was again. The faint cry of a baby. What was it that made the cry of a newborn different from that of an older infant? She winced in sympathy when the cry was disrupted by a cough. Since the incident at the Bent N' Dent two days ago, she'd been apprehensive about running any errands that would take her off the farm. Thankfully none had arisen, for Miriam would have certainly volunteered as Esther was distracted with the *boppeli*'s cold.

After a few faint murmurs, the cry quieted. Miriam visualized Esther moving from the bed to the nearby cradle. She'd take a moment to change the child, then settle into the wooden rocker to feed little Uri.

Flipping her pillow over, Miriam rested her

cheek against the cool cotton. She hoped the Zooks were getting some sleep. Newborns were up multiple times a night, but since the onset of the cold, Miriam figured Esther— and by default Isaiah—were doing more waking than sleeping. At least the other children seemed to sleep through the noise. Miriam wished she had the ability. Even as the thought chased through her mind, following closely on its heels was the realization that in a few years, after she and Levi married, she'd be waking to tend to her own infant. Her lips curved at the prospect of cuddling her child.

Seconds later, Miriam's eyes popped open when the face of the man smiling at her over the tiny head of the anticipated *boppeli* was not blond Levi Peachy, but a dark-haired Aaron Raber, his blue eyes lit with tenderness.

Miriam squeezed her eyes shut and struggled to corral her suddenly galloping heart rate. Burrowing deeper into the covers, she took measured breaths of the room's chilly air. Normally, so tired at the end of busy days, she'd eventually drop back to sleep after registering the *boppeli*'s cry. Tonight, following that disconcerting vision, her mind was as alert as if she'd consumed a pot of *kaffi*. No matter how she tried to relax—shifting her position, counting the cows in the barn, counting the spots on the Holstein cows in the barn—she couldn't return to sleep.

She shouldn't be thinking of Aaron in that way. She was marrying another man. She shouldn't be thinking of Aaron at all. Only in how his appetite contributed to the quantity of corn bread she needed to make for supper. For sure and certain, he'd been a surprise. Much different than she'd expected. *Ja*, he was arrogant, but not as much as she'd anticipated. As for irresponsibility, she'd been impressed by how hard he worked at the Zooks'. How concerned he'd been for the Hershberger boys. Her fingers curled around the covers as she pulled them up to her chin. How wonderfully comforting his hand had felt covering hers when she'd confessed about that awful time in jail and when they'd confronted Blake in the parking lot.

Another sound penetrated the darkness. Miriam jerked her head off the pillow. Whatever this was, it wasn't the baby. Holding her breath, she listened. The big house was quiet, the soft ticking of her battery alarm clock the only sound. Its glowing hands pointed to eleven o'clock. Miriam slowly exhaled. Perhaps she'd imagined it. *Wait.* There it was again—a muted burst of noise. She wouldn't have heard it if she hadn't been awake and aware.

The noise was mechanical and coming from outside. Which was odd in this part of the country, inhabited as it was by many Plain folk. Particularly in the middle of the night when most, anticipating an early morning, would be asleep. With a soft gasp, Miriam pulled the quilt over her ears. Was it Blake and his *Englisch* friends? Had they followed Aaron here? Were they going to threaten her again? Or Esther and Isaiah? The Zook children?

Jerking the covers back at the thought, she sat up. Tipping her head, she listened to determine if Isaiah or even Esther was investigating. Their room remained silent. Miriam froze when the sound erupted again. A mechanical cough, followed by silence. Tension seeped from her. It wasn't a car.

Miriam slipped off the bed. Bare toes curling on the cold floor, she crept to the frosted window, cleared a small spot and peered out. Beyond the dark farmyard, a faint light was visible from around the barn door. Someone was inside.

Hastily dressing, Miriam tiptoed to her bedroom door. If Isaiah was getting some much-needed sleep, there was no reason to wake him. Whatever it was, it shouldn't be too dangerous. Not like the fire a troubled Amish youth had started in the bishop's house recently.

Besides, Miriam thought as she stuffed her sockless feet into her black sneakers, beyond the frost in the window she'd noticed a buggy—horseless—next to the barn where Aaron usually parked. His? But that was odd, as he'd left earlier. She knew because, much to her disgust, her gaze had followed his rig down the lane.

Grabbing her winter coat from a peg by the kitchen door, she stepped outside. Below the hem of her dress, the cold of the still night nipped at her bare legs. Fresh snow sparkled like diamonds in the full moon, highlighting an odd trail across the yard that stretched from the house to the barn. Shoving her arms into her coat sleeves, Miriam followed it, snow crunching under her shoes.

Four parallel lines crossed the evening's newly fallen snow. It took her a moment to recognize the cuts as sled runners. Two sets were shallow. Empty sleds? The other two ran alongside, deep cuts made by the runners with snow matted between them, indicating whatever had been on the sleds had been very heavy. Even the boot prints along the cuts were different, with indentions suggesting the wearer had dug in on the deeper tracks to pull with force. From the direction of the footprints, someone had taken the empty sleds to the mudroom entrance of the house and transported something heavy back to the barn after the new snow had fallen that evening.

But who? And what? And why?

Her eyes on the rig, Miriam felt confident as to who. The district's *Ordnung* determined what the community's buggies looked like. To some, the rigs all looked the same. But to a keen observer, differences were visible to identify certain buggies. Having been curious about its driver, Miriam had been a very keen observer of Aaron's buggy as it had sat daily in the Zook farmyard. She recognized it now, even with an inch of snow draping it. Why was Aaron here, instead of at his home, in the middle of the night? And he'd been here for some time, as no buggy tracks trailed up the lane in the new snow.

At the man door to the barn, she jumped when the quiet was ripped by a mechanical roar, much louder here than in the house. In the brief moment it rumbled before puttering to a stop, she cracked the top of the split barn door open, cringing as the cold hinges creaked in protest, and peeked in. From their stalls, the horses swung their heads in her direction. Among them, she recognized Aaron's gelding. But where was he?

The motor rumbled again. Flicking their ears, the horses turned their heads toward an alley at the back of the barn. Stepping through the barn door, Miriam closed it behind her and cautiously proceeded in that direction. Where the alley split, with one corridor leading to the milking parlor, she turned in the other toward a gate that led to an open-air pen protected from the elements by an extension of the hayloft.

Miriam crept to the gate. Aaron stood with his back to her. The *woolie* she'd recently washed for him was pulled down over his dark hair as he bent to a task. A lantern spread a halo of light over the immediate area. Various tools were neatly lined up on an old towel that'd been laid on the dull gray concrete. The smell of exhaust slightly overrode the ubiquitous barn odors that'd greeted her when she'd entered the building. When Aaron shifted, Miriam caught sight of the object of his midnight maintenance. What he'd pulled from the mudroom to work on in the middle of a cold night was the inoperable gas washing machine.

Stifling a soft exclamation at the sight,

Miriam watched Aaron blow on his hands, presumably to warm them, before reaching into the bowels of the machine. Why was he doing this? And why now? Surely he could've found a warmer time and place to work?

Earlier in the day, his solemn gaze had lingered on her hand when she'd given him the cleaned stocking cap. Self-conscious of its rough, reddened appearance, she'd jerked it back to hide in the folds of her skirt. He'd looked from it to the hat and frowned. Now, recalling the exchange, Miriam blinked against the tears that prickled at the backs of her eyes.

Tonight's efforts might not have anything to do with her. Aaron always said he liked motors. Maybe he couldn't resist working on one. Or maybe he was doing it to gain favor with the Zooks—taking care of what was an undesirable task for Isaiah, or even doing it for Esther, out of respect for his boss's wife.

But Miriam didn't think so. She'd been the one taking care of the laundry. He was repairing it for her. She hugged her arms about her as a spark ignited in her chest. The realization that Aaron was fixing the washing machine for her in the middle of a cold night warmed her more than the jacket she wore.

As for why he was doing it here in the open

air instead of inside? A faint cloud of exhaust hung above the machine before it dissipated in the slight breeze, reminding Miriam of Aaron's admonishment regarding carbon monoxide and enclosed areas. The warning had prompted her to ask Esther about the attachment she'd noted connecting the washer to the window of the mudroom.

"Oh that." Esther had frowned at the nonfunctioning machine. "That's to vent the exhaust outside. If it ever runs again, to have exhaust."

Although tempted to thank Aaron, to share in the moment, Miriam remained silent. What would she say to this gift, one of the most thoughtful she'd ever been given? Edging away from the gate, her gaze remained on the broad back of the laboring man. One who'd refused to stay pigeonholed in the character she'd expected.

As she followed her tracks back to the house, Miriam heard the motor start up again. Subconsciously, she held her breath as it coughed a few times. When it caught and held, she slowly exhaled. The muted sound of it followed her all the way into the house. Looking back at the barn, she quietly closed the door.

Once she was snuggled back under the covers, thoughts of Aaron again intruded. This time, Miriam didn't chase them away. Instead, eyes drifting shut, she sighed and fell asleep, her lips curling into a smile.

Aaron snuck a glance at Miriam from his side of the milking parlor. Had she noticed? Probably not, since she and the children were helping in the barn this morning, as Isaiah had left early to see another dairyman about buying one of his cows. She wouldn't have had a chance to even think about the washing machine. Even if she had, she wouldn't have known by looking at it that it was repaired. The task had taken him most of the night. It would almost be worth another egg soiling his hat just to be able to show her.

The Zook children, down to two-year-old Abram, were contributing to the morning's milking in various ways. Occasionally, Aaron would do a count, just to ensure all were still present. Otherwise, while his hands worked automatically, his gaze drifted to where Miriam was milking. He'd caught her meeting his glance occasionally. When she did, she'd blush and look away.

*Ja*, he couldn't wait to show her the working machine. If a look across bony-hipped cows this morning had her blushing, what would the knowledge of what he'd done for her do? Prompt her to kiss him? His lips quirked. Their relationship had come a long way. A kiss would be much better than the snowball that'd smacked him in the face earlier in their acquaintance.

Rising from the stool, he pulled the bucket of milk from under the cow. Handing it off to Philip, Aaron released the stanchions for the set of cows on his side and herded them from the milking parlor. He opened the door to the lot, and six more cows eagerly entered and swiftly sorted themselves out into the stanchions.

Aaron was just starting to milk the first when a child's shriek came from the hayloft. His head shot up to meet Miriam's worried glance. Lurching to his feet, the stool rattled behind him as Aaron took a quick inventory of the parlor. One was missing.

"Delilah?" There was no answer to Miriam's anxious call. The other children stopped what they were doing and looked, with varied degrees of concern, to the hayloft's wooden ladder and the opening above it.

Before Miriam could rise from her stool next to the Holstein she'd been milking, Aaron launched himself toward the ladder. Hurtling bales of straw that blocked his path, he landed on the ladder three rungs up from the bottom. The rough wood biting into his hands, he scrambled to the top. Leaping across the yawning opening, he paused on the hay-strewn wooden boards.

"Delilah?" His mind raced with possible dangers found in a hayloft. Years ago, a neighbor's son had fallen down a deep hole between the bales and had been trapped in the tight space. He'd been alone at the time, so no one had known where to look for him until it'd been too late. Snakes, in search of mice, sometimes made their homes in haylofts. Although sightings of poisonous ones in this part of Wisconsin were rare, the area did have some. Even a nonvenomous bite from some of the large snakes he'd found in haylofts could lead to problems for a six-year-old.

Miriam clambered up behind him. He gave her a hand to cross the wide opening. They stood side by side, their rapid breathing the only sounds. Before them were walls of stacked bales of various heights, hay on one side, straw on the other. But no sign of a little girl.

"I found them!"

The cry was eager, not frightened or urgent. Aaron frowned at Miriam.

Magdalene's head popped up through the

hayloft opening at their feet. "Is everything all right?"

"Did she find the kittens?" Joanne's piping voice came from below. Looking down through the opening, Aaron saw her upturned face, her hands on miniature hips. "If so, I want to see them, too!"

To Aaron's immense relief, Delilah's head appeared over the crest of a mountain of straw in the depths of the hayloft. He started in her direction. As he climbed over the bales toward her, his ears picked up the mewl of kittens. "You found a batch of kittens?" He shook his head at her excited nod. He couldn't chastise the little girl for frightening them when she was so thrilled. "I didn't know they were missing."

"*Ja!* Six! We thought Lulu must've had babies somewhere, as she got skinny so fast a few weeks ago. We looked and looked all over the farm but couldn't find them. But this morning I heard them while I was helping." Carefully, Delilah lifted a hand with a little bundle of fur to where Aaron could see it. She gently set the miniature feline on his extended palm. Minute blue eyes stared back at him. The black-and-white kitten's ears were just beginning to point upward from its tiny head.

At a rustling of straw, Miriam appeared at

his side. When she saw the kitten, she made the "ooh" sound that women make at the sight of something cute and cuddly. Seeing her expression, Aaron was tempted to echo it. She looked pretty cute and cuddly to him. Wisely remaining silent, he gingerly transferred the kitten to her. Philip and Magdalene popped into view as they scrambled over the bales. Their eager gazes were on the two kittens Delilah now held, twins to the one in Miriam's hand. David was a mere step behind his siblings.

"I want to see! I want to see!" Even the mountains of straw bales between them couldn't muffle Joanne's indignant voice.

"*Gut* thing the cat was wise enough to have several." Aaron winked at Miriam. "I'll be right back." Climbing back down over the bales, he swiftly descended the ladder to the two impatiently waiting children. Abram immediately lifted his arms in an invitation— or maybe it was the toddler's command—to be picked up.

"I'll get you in a minute, buddy." Swinging Joanne into his arms, Aaron climbed up high enough on the ladder to be able to set her on the edge of the opening. He kept a hand on her as she steadied herself. Before he could let go, she was scrambling toward the others.

Dropping again to the barn floor, he picked up Abram and climbed the ladder and the bales, keeping the two-year-old in his arms even as he settled down in the huddle with the other children.

*"Ja,"* he murmured, picking up the last kitten, "Mama kitty left one for you, too, but you have to be very gentle." Holding the blurry-eyed feline in his hand, he showed the little boy how to carefully pet the baby. When Abram seemed to understand, Aaron looked over with a grin to where Miriam sat. At the warm look in her eyes, he momentarily forgot about the kitten, the boy, the hayloft, even his own name.

He was in the midst of reaching for her, the young dual burden in his lap notwithstanding, when the yowl of the kitten and an impatient bawl of a cow from below drew him to an abrupt halt. With a hard swallow and a shaky sigh, he tore his gaze from Miriam to glance around at his juvenile milking crew. "The cows are saying we need to get back to work. Let's carefully put the kittens back where we found them and finish what your *daed* expects us to do."

With Abram in his arms, he rose to his feet. Hoping for another one of her alluring gazes, he hiked an eyebrow and offered a hand to

Miriam to help her maneuver down over the bales. Instead of the hand he'd anticipated, a miniature one grasped the ends of his fingers. He looked down to see Joanne's trusting gaze. His hand curled around hers as his smile twitched to one more suited for a little girl than the nearby older one who'd been taking up a good share of his thoughts.

After ensuring all the *kinner* safely reached the barn floor, Aaron turned to help Miriam down from the loft. To his disappointment, she was already descending the final steps. Without another glance at him, warm or otherwise, she returned to the Holstein she'd been milking and took up position on the stool. With a sigh, Aaron returned to his unmilked cow as well.

But his thoughts were on the two-legged female across the alley and not the four-legged one in front of him. Why change now? He'd thought of her all night while he'd been working on the washing machine. It'd been late by the time he'd gotten the motor running to his satisfaction, so he'd spent the rest of the night in the barn. Isaiah, having seen Aaron's rig outside, had raised his eyebrows when he'd come into the barn, waking Aaron from where he'd been sleeping on a pallet he'd made with straw and the blanket from his buggy. The older man had left him with instructions for the day. Instructions that didn't include the *kinner* being late for school this morning because the hired man was thinking more of the hired girl than about getting things done in a timely manner.

Knowing milking would take longer anyway, as Isaiah was faster at milking than Miriam, Aaron increased his own speed and concentrated on anything he could to avoid thinking of the enticing woman in the barn with him. He calculated the number of cows they'd milked, how many were left to milk and how many milk cans he'd need to take to the cheese factory. Calculated how much time might pass before he could try to kiss the girl across the milking parlor's alley. And even with her earlier surprisingly warm look, how much time before she fully trusted him, if she ever would, with her disgust of lawbreakers and his…situation.

The cow's tail swatted him, stinging his face. Batting it away, he grimaced. He had to make a decision on what he was going to do about Blake. He was running out of time. Blake was a man of action, not one of patience. He liked to remind folks who was in power. With a grim expression, Aaron moved on to the next cow.

He'd taken a risk last year, hoping to break free by disappearing from the area. Blake had obviously done without him the year he'd been gone. Why not now?

Aaron looked up at the rattle of the stanchion. This particular cow was young, being milked after her first calf and obviously uncomfortable being cornered. Aaron could relate. He felt trapped in his situation. Blake had a reputation to maintain. No one quit on Blake. His previous boss reminded Aaron of something he'd read in a history book where a subject wasn't to turn his back on a king or leave the king's presence without the ruler's permission. Blake had built his kingdom. He decided when you left—*if* you left. Fear and discipline kept his empire in line. That and the example of a few who'd left and suffered extensively for it.

Feeling his tension, the young cow stomped her foot and edged away from him. Aaron forced himself to relax. He'd been good at the work he'd done at the chop shop. But he didn't think he was so good that Blake wouldn't, or couldn't, replace him.

Did Blake assume because Aaron was Plain that he was more gullible, making him easier to control? Remorse curdled in his stomach like sour milk when Aaron recalled how eagerly he'd gotten involved in something he knew was wrong. But how did he escape the repercussions of his bad decisions? Please *Gott*, let him do so before someone was hurt.

Finishing with the young cow, he released her. She quickly backed away from the stanchion and rushed out of the barn. Aaron solemnly watched her hasty exit.

There had to be some way to quit Blake's gang without leaving the area. And he'd better come up with it quick. Because if he didn't take some kind of action soon, Blake surely would.

# Chapter Ten

Miriam rinsed a glass and put it in the dish drainer. Esther was in her room feeding the *boppeli*. The older children were at school. Isaiah had taken the milk to the cheese factory. The house was quiet, the only sound the tumble of blocks from where Abram and Joanne were playing in the next room.

She washed another glass, her attention not on the breakfast dishes, but on the barn. Hoping to catch sight of Aaron? She twisted her lips. Other than mealtimes, she hadn't seen him since yesterday morning when she and the *kinner* had helped with the milking. His absence hadn't kept her from thinking about him, though. A lot. Too much. Thinking and wondering. Wondering why the sight of Levi's smile didn't make her melt the way the sight of Aaron's did. Wondering why the thought of kissing Levi didn't tempt her the way the thought of kissing Aaron did.

Heat crept up her cheeks. A hayloft might be a common place for a first kiss with a man, but who would consider doing so with six children and a batch of mewling kittens for witnesses? Who beyond her, leaning to meet Aaron more than halfway before he'd jerked back yesterday? At the memory, Miriam twisted the dishrag inside the glass until it squeaked.

So what if the man had fixed a washing machine for her? Although she'd caught his considering glances toward her, he'd never said a word about that night's work. Besides, Levi had... What *had* Levi ever really done for her? Beyond remind her frequently of her big mistake and how she needed him to guide her. To help her curtail her impulsiveness and let him be her guide in judging right from wrong, as she was obviously lacking in that capability.

Maybe she did need him. She was again falling for another charming man of shady character. Unlike Tobias, she already knew this one had participated in illegal activity. And this one, if she wasn't careful, she was very much afraid she could grow to...

"I'm a fool." She scrubbed fiercely at residual syrup on one of the children's plates. "I'm a fool mooning over a man when I already have a beau. A different one." *A safe one.* Did she want a safe beau? Her impulsive heart said no. Her mind, which had picked up the pieces scattered by her impulsive heart, firmly nodded. Reluctantly, Miriam nodded as well.

A flash of movement outside the window drew her attention. Miriam stiffened at the sight of two vehicles pulling into the farmyard. Blake and his gang? Even as fear jolted her, she realized these were not cars, but something the *Englisch* called SUVs. SHERIFF and some words in smaller print were emblazoned in black over the doors. Strangling the dishrag in her hand, Miriam watched the vehicles make a slow turn around the farmyard before pulling up close to the barn. A trim man in uniform exited each SUV.

She shrunk back from the window when they looked toward the house. The officers in Ohio had been professional and kind in their dealings with her. Her fear wasn't their fault. But the sight of the uniformed men brought back memories of shock—of panic, turmoil and Tobias's betrayal. Of shame that she'd never been able to shed. Were they coming to the house? Miriam's heart rate accelerated.

When Aaron opened the barn door and

looked out, it became obvious who they were searching for. Both officers immediately pivoted in his direction. One must've said something as, warily, Aaron stepped outside the barn and shut the door. A few moments later, he lifted his hands away from his body. The officers approached him. When one of them detached his cuffs from his belt, Miriam's hand flew to her mouth. With a glance toward the house, Aaron turned around and put his hands behind his back. As the officer began to cuff him, Miriam dashed to the door and raced outside.

An officer was opening the door to the back seat of one of the SUVs when she ran across the yard.

"What… Why?" She couldn't even voice the question.

"Please stay back, ma'am." The officer held up a hand, his voice courteous but firm.

Miriam stumbled to a halt a short distance away. "Aaron? What's going on?"

Aaron was as pale as she'd ever seen him. With a bowed head, he preceded the officer to the vehicle. When he stopped by the open back door, he looked up and straight at her. "Tell the Zooks I'm sorry." His eyes squeezed shut, his throat bobbing in a hard swallow. When he opened his eyes, Miriam bit her lip at the anguish she recognized in them, even with the SUV's hood and more between them.

"I'm so sorry, Miriam." His hoarse voice was barely discernible. The officer beside Aaron put a hand on Aaron's head. He disappeared from her sight into the back of the vehicle.

Miriam backed away, her own throat working, as the officers, following a brief nod in her direction, got into the SUVs and sedately pulled out of the yard. Watching them go, she started to shake, a reaction not from the exterior cold that buffeted her coatless body, but from a pervading chill inside her.

What had just happened? Had Aaron rejoined Blake and his gang? Yesterday he'd seemed so content. So responsible. So...appealing. Her impulsive heart had again led her astray. He was a lawbreaker. Hugging herself, she blinked against the burning at the back of her eyes. "You're a fool, Miriam. You can't trust him. And obviously, you can't trust yourself. When will you ever learn?"

Aaron felt the clanging of the door in his chest as much as his ears. Sinking onto the metal bunk, he braced his elbows on his now orange-clad knees. Lowering his head, he rested it in his hands. They said they had an eyewitness who saw him stealing a car the night before last. Aaron didn't know how he'd done it, but Blake was certainly behind the claim.

He rubbed his forehead. For sure and certain, it wasn't Blake's fault he was here, though. It was all his. He may not be guilty of this particular crime. But while he'd never lifted a car during the time he'd worked for the gang, he'd also never questioned where the cars had come from, or why he ground off or replaced vehicle identification numbers. Or helped dispose of removed parts in various ways. He hadn't wanted to know. He didn't need to ask or be told to know what he was doing was illegal.

Which was why he never said anything to defend himself today when they'd booked him, beyond an initial, feeble, "I didn't do it"— probably the litany of all who'd ever stepped into a jail cell. He hadn't argued against his circumstances as they'd fingerprinted him and taken his mug shot. His gut twisted at the thought of Miriam having gone through the same procedure after the drug incident in Ohio. And unlike him, she'd been innocent.

The only time he'd stifled a protest was when they'd taken his clothes to replace them with the orange uniform he now wore. Ironic, when for a few years, he hadn't appreciated his Plain attire and had shed it as frequently as possible. But being forced to change today, when he felt like he was stripping out of his very identity—his chosen identity—had almost buckled his knees. As had the expression on Miriam's face when they'd picked him up this morning.

He'd known if he didn't take action, Blake would. But he hadn't expected this. How did Blake know he wouldn't talk? Grimacing, Aaron answered his own question. Because he had no proof. He'd been avoiding the gang. He didn't know if they were working out of the same location, or even who was involved anymore. It would be the same he said/he said that Miriam had sat in jail for. And Blake would've had ample time to cover his tracks.

At least he was alone in his misery. Someone was in the next cell over, but other than raising his head from the metal bunk when Aaron had been ushered in, the man had folded his arms under his head and ignored him. Aaron closed his eyes. He didn't want anyone to see him like this. Not even a stranger.

He completely understood Miriam's shame when she'd confided her past. Sweat beaded down his back at the knowledge she'd witnessed his disgrace. He'd never told his family what he'd been involved in. His *daed* probably knew he'd been doing something he shouldn't be, by his lack of interest in any other work and the odd hours he'd kept. Like the nights he'd disappear once he got a call on his cell, because they tore down a car, usually within a few hours, after it'd been lifted. Miriam was the only one he'd confided anything to regarding his old job, and only because she'd been there when Blake had confronted him the night of the singing. And look how well that'd gone over with her.

After she got over her shock, she'd feel vindicated in his arrest. Knowing what she'd now think of him, saliva pooled at the back of his mouth. He shot a quick glance to the metal toilet, just in case he got sick. Although throwing up inside the jail couldn't make him feel any worse than he already did.

Hours later, lying dejectedly on the metal bed, he sat up at the clang of the heavy metal door.

"Raber." It swung open. "You're out of here."

"What?" The word burst out as, heart pounding, Aaron lurched to his feet.

"The prosecutor didn't think there was enough to keep you. Apparently the witness who'd put you at the scene of the crime and IDed you from a photo lineup didn't hold up. And someone came in to offer you an alibi for that night." The officer swung the cell door open. "Said it couldn't have been you. Said you were miles away from where the car was stolen, fixing a washing machine in a barn at the time." The man's lips twitched and the eyes above them held humor. "Which seems like an odd way to spend a late evening. Unless it was to impress a girl."

"It was," Aaron responded absently, his mind whirling. Brows furrowed, he slipped through the door the young deputy held open. Once on the other side, his shaky inhale was checked by an automatic flinch when the cell door behind him clanged shut. He was still guilty—perhaps not of this crime, but of his association with the gang from months back.

Who had provided the alibi? Had Isaiah come out to the barn for some reason that night? If he had, why hadn't he said anything? Aaron grimaced. Isaiah might've given him an alibi, but would he let him keep his job? Or would he let him go, figuring while not guilty of this incident, for someone to claim Aaron had been involved, his trustworthiness was in question.

Aaron had never been so glad to get back

into his broadfall pants and suspenders. He waited at the next secured door while the deputy glanced up at the camera above it, pressed a button and spoke to the muffled voice on the intercom. With a click, the door unlocked. The deputy opened it and ushered Aaron into the jail's public lobby. He froze in the doorway at the sight of who waited for him.

Miriam was trying to make herself as small as possible as she huddled in a corner seat. She jolted to her feet at the sight of him. Her blue eyes were enormous in a face as white as the *kapp* just visible beneath her black bonnet. Slender fingers were knotted against the front of her enveloping cloak. Even in the tangle, he could see them tremble as her eyes darted from him to the uniformed deputy. She looked more traumatized than he'd felt from spending the bleak hours in a jail cell. Heart aching for her distress, he strode a few steps into the room. Realizing his arms were lifting to wrap around her forlorn figure, he jerked to a halt, dropped one hand to his side and rubbed the back of his neck with the other.

"What are you doing here?"

Miriam shivered as if the temperature in the room matched the snowy weather outside. "I saw you in the barn that night. I know you were there at the time…they said you weren't."

Although he kept his eyes on her as he crossed the beige tiles to where she stood, Aaron was aware of the empty room surrounding them. He halted a step away. Surely she hadn't come by herself? But not only wasn't there another Plain person in the room, it was devoid of any *Englisch* as well.

"Are you alone?" His voice rose half an octave on the question.

Biting her lip, Miriam nodded. Her chin quivered.

This situation was so distressing for her; he had to get her out of here. He turned to the deputy who'd followed him into the room. "Are we…done here? Can we go?"

The young deputy, STONE engraved on a bar on his uniform, nodded and smiled. "I'm sure it's mutual, but I hope I don't see you again soon."

Aaron dipped his chin in acknowledgment. Cupping Miriam's shoulder with a light grip, he guided her toward the outer door. Under the wool of her cloak, her shoulder stiffened beneath his fingers. He bit the inside of his cheek. It was as he'd expected. Even though she'd come in for him, even though she knew he was innocent of this, she also knew he wasn't innocent of breaking the law. Still, when he held the door open for her, he stifled the urge to slip his arm the rest of the way around her shoulders—comfort he needed maybe even more than she did. Instead, his arm dropped. When they stepped outside, he almost felt like smiling for the first time that day.

"You drove my own horse and buggy in?"

A flush crept over her pale cheeks. "I asked Isaiah and Esther for time off to come. I could hardly ask them for a rig as well. Besides, I figured you wouldn't mind."

"I don't." He swallowed against the knot in his throat. "In fact, I can't thank you enough. Especially knowing how you feel about jails." This time, he gave in to his inclination and gathered her cold fingers into his grasp.

For a moment, she didn't resist. Briefly, she returned his grip before tugging her hands free and quietly hissing, "Don't give me sympathy."

Aaron blinked. He would've been angry if regret hadn't stung him more. What happened to the frail-appearing woman inside the jail? She was back to being the spitting kitten she'd been earlier in their relationship. He'd thought they'd gotten beyond that. At least he'd hoped they had.

Miriam's hands were curled into fists. "I wore a path in front of the building before I went in. And in the barn at the Zooks', before I gathered the courage to come to town."

He untied the gelding. "But you did come in."

She crossed her arms over her chest. "It wasn't so bad."

He shot her a glance. "You don't lie enough to do it well. I know what you were thinking. You were scared almost out of your shoes in there."

For a moment, he thought she was going to argue with him. Her lips firmed as she hunched a shoulder. "So?"

"So was I."

She drew a deep breath and opened her mouth as if she was going to say something. Then the air seeped out of her as if from a slowly deflating ball. "Fair is fair. I know you didn't do what you were accused of. Even though I might not agree with what you have done, you shouldn't be punished for what you haven't."

Turning, she climbed into the buggy. On the left side. Without argument. She wouldn't sit on the left side coming home from a Sunday night singing, but apparently it was more acceptable when you were picking someone up from jail? Even when she was obviously mad? Aaron shook his head. He doubted he'd ever understand women.

Releasing the gelding, he climbed up beside her. He backed the horse and quickly pulled away from the jail. The building, although neat and clean, couldn't be in his rear view fast enough. He squinted at the setting sun. If they hurried home, he wouldn't even miss a milking session. *If* he still had a job. His stomach twisted at the possibility he might not. Months ago, he would've dreaded doing what he'd considered drudgery: shoveling manure, milking twice a day, day in and day out. Now the warm comfort of the barn, the gentle lowing of the cows, the friendly camaraderie with Isaiah—well, he'd miss it.

And where would he go without it? Maybe that'd been Blake's plan. Who in the community would hire him, knowing as they surely all did that he'd been in jail? The Amish grapevine was more efficient than many *Englisch* communication systems. "I suppose the whole district knows." His voice was as low as his mood.

"*Ja.* That's how I knew why they'd arrested you." Her hands were on her lap, knotted so tightly together the knuckles were white. "Why did they think it was you?"

"They said a woman called in. Said she saw an Amish man stealing a car. She identified me in a photo lineup, probably using my driver's license picture from when I had a car. When they went to question her further, what she said apparently fell apart. I'm sure Blake was behind it. Probably bribed or threatened someone. He didn't want me in jail forever. Just wanted to shake me up a bit." Which he certainly had. If Aaron had no job, and couldn't find another one, that would pressure him even more into returning to work for his old boss.

His shoulders sagged. He wanted to slow the gelding, making the journey linger, as it was probably the last time he'd have reason to be alone with her, even snappish as she was. There was so much he was tempted to say. Not that she'd want to hear it. Particularly now. Besides, Miriam had a job, even if he didn't. "I'm guessing I need to get you back."

"You too. It's milking time."

He jerked his head in her direction. "You mean I still have a job?"

"*Ja.* Isaiah never thought you did what they said you had. He heard the motor in the barn that night, same as I. Although he didn't come out to investigate, when he went out to milk, he saw the sled tracks in the snow taking the washer back and forth. And no buggy tracks. Meaning you'd been there all evening."

Aaron was numb with relief. He shook his

head. "I didn't think about that. I just knew I had no alibi." He smiled crookedly as he studied her. "And here I thought I was being so stealthy working in the barn. I certainly didn't think about the tracks."

"They were demolished with tire tracks when the sheriff's department arrived."

Grunting, Aaron faced the road. "I understand the feeling. I was, too."

"Why didn't you tell them you were innocent?" It almost sounded like an accusation.

"I did, but it worked about as well as it did for you back in Ohio. But I'm not really innocent, am I? *Nee,* even if I never lifted a car myself, I was involved with what the gang was doing and profited from it." He scowled. "Maybe that's why I kind of felt I deserved to be where I was. I figured there was a chance justice would catch up to me sometime. I guess a bit of me was glad it finally did." He shook his head. "But not glad enough that I ever want to go back."

"If you loved it so much, why didn't you just stay with the *Englisch* and do something with cars and motors?" Miriam stared straight ahead, as if the ribbon of highway absorbed all her interest.

Shrugging, Aaron sighed. "Because I want an Amish life. It may not seem like it, but I love my family and the community. This is where I want to raise my own family. And there's a need for that kind of work. I want to start a business here. Not cars, but a lot of different types of motors are used in generators, refrigerators and so many other things the district uses to avoid connection to the *Englisch* world."

"Like washing machines?"

Was she teasing him? Aaron searched her profile but couldn't tell anything from her expression.

"I heard it finally run as I was heading back to the house. It will be helpful in getting the laundry done. I guess I haven't thanked you for that." Her voice was low.

Impulsively, Aaron reached over and covered her hands with his own. "I think you've thanked me more than enough with what you've done today."

Miriam didn't say anything, just looked down to where his hand covered hers. Her fingers twitched under his. With a wince, Aaron drew his hand away and returned it to the reins.

His stomach felt hollow. He might've retained his job. But he'd lost her trust—something much more precious.

# Chapter Eleven

Miriam turned the pancakes as Magdalene and Delilah set the table. Since the children didn't have to rush off for school, Saturday breakfasts were a little more leisurely. The door behind her opened and the men entered, bringing in with them a brisk breeze.

She pressed the spatula down on the pancakes. She hadn't talked with Aaron since the ride home last night. Upon their arrival, he'd gone straight to the barn where Isaiah had already begun the milking. Apparently things had gone well between the two men, as supper last night was as if Aaron's ordeal never occurred. The children had looked puzzled when Isaiah teased Aaron about seeing parts of the county he'd never seen and hoped never to see, to which Aaron fervently replied he hoped to never see them again either.

Miriam was relieved for Aaron. The Zooks were *gut* people. She hoped Aaron found acceptance from others in the community as well.

And from her? Last night, while her attention had remained on her plate, she'd just toyed with her food. The emotional whirlwind of the day had exhausted her. She'd felt Aaron's gaze on her a few times during the meal, but thankfully he hadn't spoken to her. She didn't know what to say to him.

Now hearing his voice with the others behind her, she grimaced. If she'd allowed him to comfort her yesterday, she'd have lost what little grasp of composure she'd had. So it was either be a shrew or a blubbering ninny for the trip. Aaron already knew she was a shrew. He didn't need to be confronted with the blubbering ninny. And Miriam didn't much want to meet her herself.

Once at the farm, she'd had a few moments before she'd needed to start supper. Going to her room, she'd pulled an extra blanket about herself. She'd crept to a corner and sank to her heels, trembling with her breath in rapid hitches. Though the tremors had finally ceased, her turmoil hadn't.

Why was she still attracted to a man who was everything she shouldn't want? Who was so wrong for her that she'd even had to pick him up from jail, a place that traumatized her? A place he might return to, based on his history and uncertain future.

Perhaps, since she couldn't trust her nature, it was time to remove herself from temptation. There were other jobs in the area. Ones where she wouldn't see Aaron Raber every day and discover there was much about him that enticed her. Jobs where she could just remember him as a lawbreaker. With a deep sigh, Miriam transferred the pancakes to a plate and turned toward the table, already crowded with the children and the two men. Her gaze immediately fastened on the younger one, currently teasing Joanne. Her heart skipped a beat at his smile. A deep breath settled it back into rhythm. *Nee,* she had to leave. Out of sight would be out of mind. She'd go as soon as Esther no longer needed her.

Miriam glanced to where her employer sat in the rocker with the *boppeli.* That didn't look to be any time soon. She bit her lip at the guilty relief that surged through her.

Thankfully, David provided a distraction from her disquiet. The six-year-old's attention was on the row of pegs inside the door where the men had just hung their outerwear. "*Mamm,* you said we'd go to the hat shop and get a new hat for me. That was days ago."

A wince rippled over Esther's tired features. Nestling Uri closer, she tried to get the infant to eat. At the weak cough that emitted from the blanketed child, Miriam doubted the worried mother was successful.

"You've been wearing my old one. What's wrong with it?"

"It's got a hole in it, Philip, and it's too small for me now. Abram can have it."

"It's a straw one. You can wait until spring to get a new one."

David didn't want to hear advice from his older brother. "You get a new hat whenever you need one. Besides, *Mamm*?" With a plaintive voice, he looked for reinforcements. "You said I could?"

Esther lowered her head over the infant she cuddled. The woman was exhausted. With the *boppeli*'s progressing cold, she was getting up even more frequently during the night. It made Miriam glad of the help she could provide taking care of the rest of the children.

Perhaps there was something she could do now. Catching Esther's eye when the woman raised her head, Miriam hiked her eyebrow and touched her hand to her chest. Esther nodded in obvious relief.

"Maybe Miriam would like to get out of the

house for a bit. How would you like to go to the shop with her?"

Setting the plate of pancakes on the table, Miriam turned to the young boy. "*Ja.* I'd love to go. But you might have to show me where it is, as I haven't been there yet."

"I know where it is. I'll show you," Philip offered.

"It's my hat. I'll show her." David left the table to scramble up on the bench beneath the peg on the wall that held his coat.

Miriam felt a tug on her dress. She looked down to see Joanne with a small hand fisted in the fabric. "Can I go too?"

Miriam looked past the little girl to see Magdalene and Delilah's hopeful faces. Abram had already run after his brother and was attempting to climb onto the bench as well.

"Back to the table." Isaiah's directive brooked no argument. The boys hustled to return to their chairs. Isaiah pondered his wife and youngest son with a solemn expression for a moment before looking around the table at his older *kinner.* His lips curved slightly. "Seems like everyone is ready to get out of the house for a bit. I don't know why—you leave it every day for school. But if you're all going, you first need to eat breakfast."

Plates of food were quickly passed, followed by the scrape of forks on dinnerware as several small heads bent to the task. In no time at all, the pancake stack was decimated. The *kinner* were scrambling from the table to carry their plates to the sink. Miriam used the accelerated pace as an excuse to keep her head down during this meal as well before she, too, sprang up from the table. She and the girls had most of the dishes finished when she heard the slide of a chair being pushed back, followed by Aaron's voice.

"Shall I harness Esther's mare for the trip?"

"*Ja.* Put a blanket on her. And Miriam, don't linger too long. It looks like there's some weather coming in."

Coat hanging by one arm, David pulled the door open. "I'll go help Aaron get the rig ready." Before anyone could respond, the door swung shut behind him. It swung open and shut a few more times in the next few moments as others followed him out the door. Miriam quickly crossed to where the collection of winter garb was rapidly dwindling from the pegs on the wall. She picked up Abram before he could express his growing frustration and held him so he could reach his own coat. Setting him on the bench, she helped him into it.

When he raced out the door as well, Miriam stopped by the chair where Esther slowly rocked the baby. "Will you and Uri be all right while we're gone?"

Esther squeezed her eyes closed and compressed her lips when the infant emitted another cough. Miriam winced at the sound. "*Ja.* Isaiah's here. I think in the meantime, I'll run hot water in the bathroom and sit in there with Uri. Maybe the steam will help his cough." She touched a finger to the child's flushed cheek. "Although I hesitate to make him warmer, as I'm pretty sure he has a fever."

"We'll be back soon. Do you need anything else while we're out and about?"

Reaching up with the hand not cuddling the infant, Esther grasped Miriam's fingers. "*Nee.* I just thank you for helping me fulfill a promise." Upon releasing her grip, she pushed up from the chair, provided Miriam with some money for the hat and headed for the bathroom. Securing the funds, Miriam collected her cloak and bonnet and followed the parade that'd earlier exited the house.

Aaron was backing Esther's mare between the buggy shafts when Miriam crossed the trampled snow of the barnyard. He looked over at her approach before glancing pointedly at the children climbing into the buggy.

"That's a lot of help for buying a hat."

Miriam told herself the stimulating shiver that ran through her was from the wind whisking around her legs and not from his warm gaze. One she wanted to respond to.

"Well, no one volunteered to stay behind. Besides," she added solemnly, "I think Esther was ready for a bit of quiet. She's worried about little Uri."

Aaron's expression grew grim as well. He threaded the lines through the storm front of the buggy and turned back to her. Another shiver ran through Miriam when he offered his gloveless hand to help her into the buggy. After a moment's hesitation as she regarded his bare palm, Miriam placed hers in its grasp. As she climbed up the step, the horse wasn't the only thing that was hitched. Her breathing did as well at his touch. She scowled. Still, instead of swiping her hand down the front of her cloak to erase the feeling, she curled it into a gentle fist for a few seconds before collecting the lines. *Oh, Miriam, what's the matter with you? He's a lawbreaker. One such as he put you in jail. He shouldn't affect you this way.*

Aaron poked his head into the buggy's open door. "I look forward to seeing your new hat, David." Nestled under blankets in the back seat, the boy beamed. Aaron turned his attention to Miriam. "Do you know where you're going? Emma Beiler made the hats before I left. I assume she still does."

Philip leaned forward from where he sat on the far side of Miriam. "I'll show her where."

"I knew I could count on you." With a nod and a tap on the side of the buggy, Aaron stepped back. Miriam slid the door closed and directed the horse down the lane. *Gut* thing the mare knew the way, as Miriam's attention was on the rearview mirror and the man watching them drive away.

Philip was a *gut* navigator. A while later she followed the children into a side door of what had been, according to Philip, an *Englisch* two-car garage next to a little house on a small farm. The shop couldn't have been any tidier. A treadle sewing machine was nestled under one window. Shelves with hats of all sizes, a mixture of straw and black felt ones, lined the walls. A faint hint of dried straw greeted her, as did the proprietress, a woman Miriam remembered seeing at church.

"My goodness, what a lively crew you have." Emma Beiler, a petite woman with dark hair just beginning to thread with grey, had an engaging smile. Miriam found herself automatically responding to it. "Are you all looking for hats?"

"Just me." David pointed his thumb at his chest.

"Then we'll need to find a very special one for you. Winter felt or summer straw?"

David's eyes lit at the sight of the black wool felt hats. He sighed. "A summer straw. Philip's old felt hat still fits me and it doesn't have a hole in it like the straw one. Yet."

"Can't have a hat with a hole in it. At least, not more than the one for your head to fit through." Emma led David to a section with smaller hats. The other *kinner* trailed in her wake.

Miriam was thrilled to discover they weren't the only customers in the shop. She crossed the linoleum floor to where her previous employer, Rachel Raber, and her husband, Ben, stood next to a shelf of black winter hats. Both Rabers had a *boppeli* in their arms as Ben shifted through the options. Automatically, Miriam lifted her arms for one of the babies. With a smile, Rachel handed Amelia over.

"Oh, how they've grown! It seems like forever since I've seen them." She stroked a finger down the *boppeli*'s petal-soft cheek.

Ben smiled at Eli, cradled in his arm. "Won't be long before they'll be out helping me with chores."

Rachel rolled her eyes. "Let's get them walking first. Or maybe even crawling."

They all glanced over when the door to the shop opened. Seeing Aaron step into the room, Miriam caught her breath as her pulse immediately doubled its cadence. When he paused after shutting the door, his eyes on the couple with her, she forgot to exhale.

She knew the two brothers had patched up their relationship after Aaron had returned to find Ben married to the woman he'd assumed he would wed. But other than church, when in the crowd it was easy to avoid someone if choosing to do so, had he ever had to confront his *bruder*'s entire family? At the sight of his face, it was obvious the answer was no.

Aaron's hand tightened on the doorknob. He was tempted to jerk the door back open and dash outside. Granted, he'd seen Ben several times since he'd returned and even been to his place to help him with projects. He'd seen Rachel since his explosion at finding her already wed when he'd come back to marry her. On Sunday mornings, he had looked across to the women's benches to see her and the blanket-wrapped bundles she and a woman sitting beside her had held. Had nodded to her across the way at socials. But seeing them all together? *Nee*, he'd been able to dodge that.

This could've been his family. His *fraa*.

His *kinner*. But what had his heart pounding was the sight of Miriam with a *boppeli* in her arms. For a moment, he didn't see anyone else. He jerked his gaze away to take in Rachel. His previous girlfriend was still beautiful. He loved her. But as a sister, not a wife. His gaze pulled back to Miriam. This... this was the woman he would want to share a child with—a family with. This was the woman he could love...for a lifetime.

With a hard swallow, he released the doorknob and strolled across the room. "I don't think you're going to find a hat in here that will fit them. At least not yet."

"Maybe not yet, but the time's coming soon. And he won't be wearing hand-me-downs like I did." Ben grinned at him. Then he scared him to death. Shifting the sleeping babe from where he was secured in one arm, he handed him toward Aaron. "Want to hold him?"

Aaron gripped the fabric of his pants, still cool from his fast trip over, with tight fingers. "I... I've never held one before. You sure you trust me with him?"

"*Ja.* I know you can do anything you put your mind to."

Aaron's breathing shallowed as Ben transferred his nephew to him. He gazed with wonder at the babe in his arms. He'd never seen a face so tiny. Or so precious. He glanced at Miriam and his breathing stopped altogether. Her expression caused his fingers to tighten on the soft blanket. He cupped a gentle hand around a tiny foot he'd discovered.

He wanted a Raber baby. His baby. Her baby. But how could a woman love you when she didn't trust you? With a rueful smile, he handed the baby back to Ben. "Let me know when he's old enough to learn how to play baseball."

"I'm sure you'll be a big part of his life long before then."

"*Ja*, the example of what not to do." There was a spattering of laughter from where the children were congregated. Aaron glanced in their direction before gripping his brother's shoulder. "It's great to see you. If you don't mind, though, I need to grab a moment with Miriam while the *kinner* are still distracted."

With a frown, Miriam followed him to a far corner of the store.

"What is it?"

"Isaiah wanted me to let you know before you and the *kinner* got home to an empty house. Little Uri turned worse. They've hired an *Englisch* driver and are taking him straight to the hospital in Portage."

Miriam's eyes rounded.

"Isaiah doesn't know when they'll be back.

He was hoping you'd take care of the *kinner* until then."

"Of course!"

"I found one!" David trotted over with both hands atop the hat perched on his head. "Can I get it?"

Sharing a look with Miriam, Aaron murmured, "I'll tell the boys," before bending to David with a smile. "Miriam will buy it for you and we'll all head home. How would you and your *breider* like to ride with me? We'll see how fast my horse can go. Maybe race the girls home."

David needed no further suggestions. He dashed across the store to tell his siblings of the plan. In no time at all, the hat was purchased and they'd waved their goodbyes before piling into the buggies.

On the ride home, at the boys' urging, they'd soon left the girls' buggy far behind. Aaron told the boys of their parents' trip with baby Uri as fat snowflakes began to splatter on the storm front. As they absorbed the news, his attention remained not on the changing weather, but on the rig that was diminishing in the distance.

No matter how fast he raced, he couldn't outrun his feelings. He was in love with Miriam. Who considered him a criminal.

# Chapter Twelve

That afternoon, the milking crew was again Miriam and the Zook children. Although the children investigated and chattered over the growth of the kittens in the loft, worry about their parents and baby *bruder* subdued them during the rest of the chores. When they were finished, Miriam herded them inside the house, promising hot chocolate while she fixed supper. Preparing the meal took twice as long, as she repeatedly went to the window to see if Aaron had returned from his two-mile round trip to the phone shack in the blowing snow to see if there was any news from the Zooks.

She spun toward the door when he stepped through, bringing a miniature blizzard into the kitchen with him.

"Anything?"

He stomped the snow off his feet. "*Ja*. Isaiah had left a message. The hospital is keeping Uri at least overnight. Something called RSV. They're giving him oxygen and extra fluids and he's doing much better. They'll stay there with him until he's released." Aaron brushed snowflakes from his dark hair. "With the weather, they wouldn't be able to get home tonight anyway." He glanced around the empty kitchen and frowned. "The *kinner* doing all right?"

"*Ja*. They're in the other room playing board games. I… I figured that was okay."

He nodded, his gaze never leaving hers. "*Gut* idea."

Miriam knotted her fingers. Now that the urgency of the situation was reduced, she felt awkward. She took a deep breath. It was only awkward if she let herself feel that way. Everything else still needed to be put aside while they did what was necessary for the children.

When she let worries and judgments go, it became comfortable, too comfortable, to have him across the table with the children surrounding them. She tried to again corral her heart, but it greedily absorbed the banter and laughter, led by Aaron, whom she knew was intentionally distracting the children. She bit the inside of her cheek. She was afraid this attraction to Aaron was like something packed into a too-small box. Once it was out, it would be nearly impossible to stuff it all back in and put the lid on again.

Aaron hadn't wanted to leave her alone that evening with the children. When the *kinner* were heading to bed after playing board games and cracking walnuts, he'd looked out the window and pronounced the weather not fit for man or beast, so he'd just stay with the beasts and sleep in the barn.

Miriam was more comforted than she wanted to admit, to either him or herself. She was also relieved to have the children around for distraction. Otherwise, she found way too much distraction with Aaron. His smile, his tender look when he'd tucked Joanne and little Abram into their beds. His broad shoulders as he pulled a sled and a toboggan up the hill.

They'd promised the children that if the storm ceased by morning, they'd take them sledding after milking. It had, and now she watched Aaron climb the hill under the blue bowl of the sky, so bright on the glistening snow it almost hurt the eyes. Beyond him, sledding paths lay like ribbons embroidered on the white fabric of the hill. Some extended farther than others. With the lighter weights of the children, paths ended where the hill leveled out and the snow became deeper.

The four oldest Zook children frolicked in Aaron's wake, pitching snowballs at each other and pouncing in the snow like puppies. Miriam's lips twitched when Delilah plopped down on the sled to catch a ride up the steep incline. Instead of being irritated by the additional load, Aaron's white teeth flashed in a smile before he turned to say something to the little girl. Miriam couldn't hear what was said, but Delilah turned to lie on her stomach and paddle her arms like she was using them to assist in the climb.

He was so *gut* with them. And with her. Watching his ascent, despite the chill flushing her cheeks, Miriam glowed inside like the bright sun above.

The storm had left deep sparkling snow covering the countryside, blanketing ditches and roads. It'd be a while before the highways, much less the country roads, were dug out enough for the Zooks to be able to get home—if little Uri was ready to do so. Whatever happened was *Gott*'s will, but Miriam prayed that His will was for the little one to quickly recover.

In the meantime, she and Aaron made a surprisingly good team.

*It's only temporary.* This "playing family" was just a small slice of time with him. She couldn't have the whole pie. It was never good to consume the whole pie just because you liked the taste of it. *Remember that, Miriam. The Zooks will be back soon. And you have someone else you're planning to be a wife to.* Someone she hadn't thought about for hours. Or had it been days?

Pivoting from the view of the approaching children, and particularly from the man leading them, she focused her attention on where Joanne was teaching little Abram to make snow angels. Their mittens and boots were encrusted with snow. It reminded Miriam of her own cold feet. If she was feeling the chill, and she'd been climbing the hill like a mountain goat, the children were also probably getting cold. Although they wouldn't admit it. But there were ways around that.

"I'm next!" Joanne plunked herself down onto the wooden slats of one of the sleds parked at the top of the hill. Snow dusted her navy scarf and lay like scales covering her corduroy jacket. Her cheeks were rosy with the cold, but her smile was as wide as the handles that protruded from both sides of the Flexible Flyer.

"Of course you are." After brushing chunks

of snow off her mittens, Miriam grabbed the twine attached to the sled and pulled it closer to where the hill dropped away. The older children were capable of sledding on their own, but she and Aaron had been taking turns with the youngest ones.

"How about one last trip and then inside for some hot cocoa?"

"With marshmallows?" Joanne scrambled to her feet to give Abram a hand up from his miniature angel.

"I think that can be arranged."

They watched the others cavorting as they climbed the hill. Joanne sighed.

"I'm going to marry Aaron when I grow up." She squinted up at Miriam. "That is, if you don't marry him first."

Miriam opened her mouth. All that came out was a cloud of condensation in a huff of exhalation. Joanne looked up at her with guileless eyes. She wanted to deny the little girl's statement. But wasn't that what she'd been fantasizing about?

She forced a smile. "I won't be marrying him. But I'm sure he'll make a *gut* husband." And he would. But not for Joanne, who'd surely get over him by the time she reached marrying age. Not for Rachel, who had gotten over him. And not for Miriam, who didn't know if she ever would.

Joanne bounced over to the quintet who'd just topped the crest of the hill. "Miriam said one more trip and then we'll go in for hot cocoa!"

Miriam held her breath, hoping the little *maedel* didn't say anything more about what Miriam had said. Thankfully, Joanne was more concerned about the final sledding trip than about Aaron as husband material.

"Who's going to ride what?" Aaron pulled the sleds and toboggans around so they were perched on the edge of the slope, facing downhill.

Eight-year-old Philip shared a glance with his older sister before turning to Aaron with a cheeky grin. "Why don't you take Miriam for a ride?"

Miriam's smile froze at the boy's words. "Oh, that's quite all right. I'm perfectly capable of going down by myself. Or not by myself. I'll give Abram a ride. He hasn't taken as many trips." She couldn't voice her protests fast enough.

"Abram can ride with me." Miriam narrowed her eyes at the impish smile that accompanied Magdalene's offer. It was too similar to the one the girl's *mamm* had worn when she'd arranged for Aaron to give Miriam a ride home from the Sunday night singing. Crouching, the girl opened her arms. Abram, fickle creature, toddled from Miriam's side over to his older sister. The girl's grin widened when she lifted him up to her hip. "Besides, maybe with the two of you on the sled, the weight will make it go farther and cut a longer path for us."

Philip echoed the thought. "That'd be great!"

Unable to come up with a way to gracefully decline, Miriam glanced at Aaron. His smile was as wide as the nearby gate. No help there. Crossing her arms over her chest, she hoped the action would suppress the excitement that had immediately percolated through her at the thought of joining him on a ride down the hill. Excitement she shouldn't be feeling. Any thrill at physical closeness with a man needed to be reserved for Levi.

Miriam's lips twitched at the thought of anything regarding Levi being exciting. It was like saying plain oatmeal was shoofly pie. And why was she having such a major internal debate about a short ride down the hill? They wouldn't even be alone on the return climb, as at least some of the children would be walking up with them.

She could handle this. She cocked her head toward Aaron. "Did she just call us heavy?"

"Couldn't have been referring to you. I'm sure you're as light as a feather. The sled won't even know you're on it. You'll float right over the top of the snow."

Miriam rolled her eyes. Taking a deep breath, she approached where he stood with one of the toboggans. His blue eyes sparkled under the dusting of a few flakes of snow caught in his dark lashes. He regarded her with a raised eyebrow, the twine of the sled wrapped in one hand. "Your choice. Front or back."

Some choice. If she sat in back, she'd have to wrap her arms around his chest. If she sat in front, her back would be pressed against it with his limbs wrapped around her. Miriam's fingers clenched inside her mittens. A quick glance determined that Aaron and all the children, their cheeks red with cold and exercise, were watching her with varying degrees of patience.

She was acting like a ninny. She'd gone sledding in Ohio. With boys her age. She'd ridden with her brothers as well. Even as they'd tried to make the trips as frightening as possible, she'd survived by bracing her hands on the side of the sled. Which is what she'd do today.

"I'll be back here."

With a knowing grin, Aaron gave her a nod and settled onto the sled. Miriam eyed the narrow area on the wooden slats that remained behind him. The toboggan had looked a lot bigger before his tall form took up all the space. Warily, she positioned herself on what was left.

Feeling like she was going to fall off the end before they even got started, she scooted forward a fraction of an inch and found herself pressed against his broad back. Her vaporized breath wafted past the lobes of his ears, visible below the rolled-up border of his stocking cap.

Aaron turned his head and it puffed against his cheek. "Are you ready back there?"

Before Miriam could inhale a shaky breath to agree, a firm pressure on her back launched them forward. She squeaked when the sled jolted over the crest. A chorus of children's laughter trailed behind as she and Aaron plunged down the hill.

Aaron must've been as startled as she at their abrupt departure. The sled tilted from side to side as it careened downward. Shrieking, Miriam flung her arms around his waist. The soft ridges of his corduroy coat rubbed under her cheek. Her nose was pressed against the dark hair that curled from underneath his hat. The wind stung her eyes. As everything was just a white blur anyway, she closed them and tightened her grip. Snow crunched under the sled, the sound changing when it raced over an occasional lightly covered rock, or jerked on impact of one of the many frozen cow pies that dotted the hillside pasture.

Miriam opened her eyes as they gradually slowed. Just when she thought they'd make it down safely, the sled swerved. Tipping, it dumped them into a drift.

Laughing was difficult with a mouthful of snow. And impossible with Aaron's touch on her cheeks as he brushed the snow off with a gloveless hand. Her eyes looked into his from inches away. His fingers paused, shifting to gently cup her jaw as his head dipped closer. Miriam angled her chin upward. Their vaporized breaths mingled. At the look in his eyes, she forgot to breathe.

"Whee! I told you we'd go farther if you two went down together." Philip, David and Joanne slid to a halt beside them on the second toboggan, with the others following closely behind on the other sleds.

Their noses brushed and their lips…almost. She and Aaron stared at each other with wide eyes until he fell back into the snow.

"Can we go again?" Having ducked her head to hide her furious blush, Miriam didn't know which of the children made the request.

"I don't know about you, but I'm getting pretty chilly." Aaron's voice cut through the crisp winter day. "Did I hear something about hot cocoa a little bit ago?"

Forget chilly. Heat seared Miriam clear down to her toes.

"Then how about a quick game of Fox and Goose?" Philip was always reluctant to go inside.

The game was seldom quick, but Miriam willingly latched on to anything to abandon the current situation. She lurched to her feet. "Sounds *gut*. Last one up the hill is the fox." Grabbing the twine of the sled on which Abram still sat, she charged up the hill. By the time she reached the top, the redness of her cheeks could be attributed to exertion and not embarrassment.

While Aaron put the sleds away, she and the children found a large untouched patch of snow. With Miriam as their leader, they shuffled in single file, laying out an intersecting trail.

"Looks like I'm the fox." Aaron jumped into the track, making sure to leave a blank section of white between the trail and any disturbed snow. He'd intentionally been last up the hill. The children preferred not to start out being the one who chased and he…he needed the time to regain his equilibrium after the moment with Miriam. Although a trip up Mt. Everest probably wouldn't be long enough for him to fully regain it.

The children—the geese—scattered over the trail that'd been laid.

"Where's the den?"

"Oh, we haven't made it yet."

To his satisfaction, Miriam still looked more than a bit unsettled. *Gut.* She'd almost kissed him. He'd almost kissed her first, but to his delight and wonder, she'd been ready to meet him at least halfway. Maybe he still had a chance. He could do a lot of things with just a little chance.

"Let me help you." They stomped out a circular area right off the trail in a blank piece of snow. "Foxes use dens. Geese roost in water or marshes. I don't know why they call the secure place for geese to go in this game a den."

Miriam looked around the small area they'd just tramped out. "Doesn't look much like a marsh. What do you want to call it? A cell?" Her hand flew to her mouth as she stared at him from across the short distance.

Aaron went still. "*Ja*. Cells are certainly secure. But they would be more for trapping the geese inside instead of keeping them safe from what's outside." He swallowed. "But I can see it as a jail cell. It's small. Cold." He held her gaze for the first time that afternoon, the cold permeating through him. "I know what you're thinking."

Miriam clasped her mittened hands under her chin. "*Nee*. I don't think you do."

Her lips pressed into a thin line. Aaron sighed. He'd been so close to kissing them. And now, would he ever again have the chance?

"Are you ever going back?"

"No." He shook his head. "To the one who caused my stay in the…den, definitely not. To being in the den? I certainly hope not, but that depends on whether any of my foolish past deeds place me there. If they do, I'll face the consequences for the mistakes I've made."

She nodded slightly, her lips now curved into a gentle smile. "That's what I needed to know."

Did that mean what he hoped it meant?

"Hey! Are we going to get something going here or not?" Philip yelled from a safe distance away on the trail.

"Are we?" Aaron blocked the entrance to the den, his intent gaze still on Miriam.

She brushed past him, her whisper no more than the condensation of breath, but he heard it and it made all the difference. "It looks like it."

Giddy with joy, Aaron was unsteady enough on his feet that it was a challenge to tag any of the children, or evade little Abram, who kept running toward him instead of away. And the one he wanted to chase, the one he wanted to catch—well, that was a whole different game.

The snowstorm had given him a slight reprieve. Even if he wanted to, Blake couldn't get to him until the roads were cleared. In the meantime, Aaron needed to find some way to be able to stay in the district without working for his old boss. Then he'd tell Blake he was done.

And after that, Aaron determined as he watched a laughing Miriam run with one of the children, he'd get involved in another, much happier union.

# Chapter Thirteen

Miriam refolded the letter and slid it through her fingers, deepening the creases. The Zooks had returned a few days ago. After a short stay in the hospital, Uri was thankfully on the mend from his bout with the respiratory virus. The roads were cleared from the storm. As for her and Aaron, although they didn't have time alone together, they were sharing secret glances and smiles. Glances and smiles Miriam dared hope might lead to other things.

That is, until Gideon dropped by and brought the letter for her on his way to work. In unhurried Gideon fashion, it had arrived days ago. Days she would've liked to have had to stop Levi from making the trip he'd surely already started.

Leaning her forehead against the kitchen cabinet, she closed her eyes, the words of the letter already regrettably imprinted in her mind. Levi was coming to visit, although his main purpose was to take her back with him. He'd decided as they'd reached an agreement and were both baptized, and as weddings were now held year-round instead of after harvest season, they could be married as soon as possible once their intent was published in their home church. Besides, he now had a house of his own and he was ready for a housekeeper.

"Something wrong?"

Straightening, Miriam opened her eyes at Esther's question. "*Ja*. But it's of my own making." And it was. She'd knowingly encouraged Levi's pursuit—encouraged it with her head and not her heart, after the shame of her situation with Tobias. Now, not even her head wanted it. And certainly not her heart. What was she going to do with him? She could hardly tell him that when he was coming all this way.

"I...um...might have a visitor."

"Oh! How lovely. Will you be wanting some time off?"

"Oh *nee*! I mean, not with you and Uri just getting back and all."

Esther raised her eyebrows. "I see. Well, you're welcome to invite the...young man?"

She smiled at Miriam's reluctant nod. "…over for supper."

Miriam smiled feebly in return. Seeing Levi right now was the last thing she wanted. She put a hand over her churning stomach. *Nee*, the last thing she wanted was to have Levi and Aaron sitting down to the supper table together.

Aaron shut the door to the milk room after Isaiah came through. Turning toward the house, his gaze narrowed on the silhouette of a rig parked next to it. "Who's that?"

"Don't know. Esther didn't say she was expecting anyone. Maybe someone came over to see the *boppeli*?"

"At supper? Seems an unusual time to visit a *boppeli*."

"One way to find out." Isaiah clamped his hand on Aaron's shoulder. "Let's go see."

Isaiah tilted his head as they approached the buggy. "Looks like Gideon Schrock's. Maybe he's hoping for a *gut* meal instead of fixing something for himself. When he coaxed Miriam up from Ohio, I think he was intending she'd be taking care of him instead of taking care of every new *boppeli* in the district."

Aaron didn't care what Miriam's *bruder*'s

motives had been when he'd convinced her to come to Wisconsin; he was just glad, more and more lately, that Gideon had. Since the Fox and Goose game, there hadn't been an opportunity for time alone with Miriam, but he was learning to be a patient man. His lips twitched. If he was going to live with the mercurial Miriam, he needed to be.

There was no question of Aaron joining in the family's supper, nor of him staying overnight in the barn where Isaiah had helped him fix up a cozy area. The situation worked out well for Aaron. He was easily on hand for early morning milkings. No more cold dark rides to and from his parents' place—rides on roads which he figured Blake's gang would be patrolling. Thankfully, they hadn't bothered his folks. It was one thing for them to stop him on the road, but something else for the rogue *Englischers* to drive into an Amish farmyard and approach the house. As long as he stayed put, they'd have a harder time finding him, giving him more opportunity to come up with a solution.

He stepped into the house, expecting to see Miriam's *bruder*. But it wasn't Gideon sitting at the table beside a flushed Miriam. It was a blond-haired stranger.

A stranger to him. Obviously not a stranger to Miriam.

Aaron ground his teeth at the sight. Jerking his jacket off, he stabbed it and his *woolie* onto the peg by the door.

Isaiah raised his eyebrows and glanced at the couple sitting at the table. "Who do we have here?" he called jovially as he shed his own coat and hat.

Esther was bringing serving dishes to the table. "This is Levi Peachy, a friend of Miriam's. He came all the way from Ohio to see her."

On his way to the bathroom to wash up, Aaron halted. Wheeling, he stared at the neat *kapp* pinned to Miriam's golden hair. Under the curling tendrils below the *kapp*, a blush crept up the back of her slender neck. Some man had come to see her? All the way from Ohio? She'd never mentioned she had a beau there—other than the one who'd gone to prison. He glared at the back of the interloper's head until he saw Magdalene, hands full of cutlery, stop on her way to the table to give him a funny look.

Pivoting, he strode to the bathroom and wrenched on the faucet. Clenching the bar of soap in his hands, he caught a reflection of himself in the small mirror Isaiah used for shaving. No wonder Magdalene had stared at him. He startled himself by how fierce he looked. Miriam was contrary enough that if he went out there spitting nails about her... visitor, she'd only blame him for being a jerk.

Soaping up, he concentrated on relaxing his jaw. What'd been the name of the fellow who'd gone to prison? Something with a *T*. For *trouble*. So who was this *Levi*? Brooding in the bathroom wouldn't help him find out. Drying his hands, Aaron tried a smile. It resembled more of a grimace. It was the best he could do.

Stepping back into the room, he called with false heartiness, "A friend all the way from Ohio. So, where are you staying?" If it was here, it better be in the barn with him. He knew of a *gut* place for the visitor. In the gutter of the milking parlor.

"I'm staying with Miriam's *bruder*, Gideon, where I thought Miriam would be. Although he seemed surprised when I arrived." Levi smiled at Esther. "He's not near the housekeeper you are. Cleanliness is next to Godliness."

"Oh, I can't take credit for the housekeeping. That's all Miriam. She's been taking care of the children and the house for the past while since I had little Uri."

The man gave Miriam a smug smile. "I know Miriam will make a wonderful house-keeper. I look forward to it."

Reaching the table, Aaron froze. When he felt capable of moving, he turned his head to give Miriam a narrow-eyed glare.

She flushed an even darker red before she dropped her gaze.

"Here scamp, let me trade places with you tonight." Lifting Abram from his seat, Aaron settled the boy into the chair where he usually sat and plunked himself down in Abram's spot. Right next to Miriam.

As he passed the potatoes, he leaned closer to mutter in her ear. "Aren't you supposed to be the one helping instead of being served?"

"I tried. Esther wouldn't let me."

"When has someone not 'letting you' ever stopped you before?"

"It stops me when she's my employer!" Miriam hissed back.

All eyes around the table, large and small, were on them. The faces wore a variety of expressions: puzzlement from the children; barely suppressed smirks from the adult Zooks; and a frown from the stranger. Under the table, Miriam stepped on Aaron's foot. Hard.

Aaron took a bite. As forcefully as he was chewing, he could've been eating cowhide.

"I came up to have Miriam return with me. That is, if she's completed her position with you. Responsibility is such an important trait."

Choking, Aaron jerked his arm at the man's words. His glass tipped over, knocking water into Magdalene's lap. Bug-eyed, the girl lurched to her feet. Aaron jumped up as well. "I'm sorry. I'll take care of it." Shoulders locked with tension, he strode to the sink for towels. At Esther's words behind him, they loosened slightly.

"Oh, I can understand why you'd want her to return. But…with us just having gotten back from the hospital with little Uri, I'm afraid we aren't ready to let her go yet."

When Aaron returned to the table, Esther's gaze was on him. Her eyes twinkled. Vigorously, he mopped up the water on and under the table. Why anyone would be amused at the situation was beyond him. Unless it was Miriam. Had she planned on stringing him along? Hooking him like a hapless trout before tossing him back when she'd decided he didn't meet her standards? He shot a glance at her before he returned the sopping towels to the sink. She didn't look amused. She looked…cornered.

*Ach*, if she felt cornered now, it'd be nothing compared to when he'd get her alone later.

\* \* \*

After supper, Levi Peachy sat and visited with Isaiah, watching and making judgmental comments while the children played games on the floor nearby. While his ears were on the men's conversation, at their urging, Aaron had played with the children. Any time Levi made a pious comment, Aaron contradicted it.

The *kinner* went to bed. The Ohio man droned on. He wasn't ever going to leave. And if he wasn't, Aaron wasn't either. It took a jaw-cracking yawn from Isaiah for the visitor to finally rise from his chair.

"Miriam, walk with me to the porch." It was a pronouncement rather than a request.

Aaron rose to his feet as well. "Time I headed out, too. Early milking tomorrow." Isaiah hiked an eyebrow, as if to say, "you think?"

He noted with satisfaction that Miriam didn't put on her coat before following Levi out the door. A moment later, coat and hat in hand, Aaron stepped outside. He stood on the porch a few feet from the couple as he slowly put them on. When Miriam began rubbing her hands up her arms to keep warm, Levi gave Aaron a look of disgust and said his farewell. A very chaste farewell, Aaron was glad to see.

Side by side, she and Aaron watched him

get into the buggy. Levi had barely started down the lane when Aaron turned and glared at Miriam.

"You never said you had a beau."

Hunching a shoulder, she glared back. "You never asked."

"You certainly didn't act like you had one." Shrugging out of his coat, he wrapped it around her.

"Oh, and how was I supposed to act? I hit you with a snowball and an egg. What was I supposed to throw next, a rock?"

"You looked at me with…warm eyes," he accused.

"Warm eyes? What's that supposed to mean?" she retorted, but a flush bloomed on her cheeks.

His voice dropped to a whisper. "You looked like you cared. You almost let me kiss you."

She ducked her chin into his coat.

Aaron sighed. She'd certainly given off "stay back" and "beware" vibes when they'd first interacted. But he'd assumed it was because she didn't like him. Then. And they'd gone beyond that. Far beyond. At least he thought so. Maybe he was seeing what he wanted to see because *his* feelings had changed. The re-alization chilled him. Maybe he did need a rock this time.

He shrugged his shoulder. "He doesn't deserve you." *Neither do I*, he wanted to add as he watched her eyes close a moment as she huddled inside his coat.

Taking it off, she handed it back to him. "Well." Her response was equally subdued. "I deserve him."

# Chapter Fourteen

"It's my day off and here I am, still doing woodworking."

Aaron recognized Gideon's voice as he approached the framed-in doorway that'd been cut into the inside wall of the house. When Miriam had mentioned to Esther this morning that her brothers were working on an addition to Samuel's house that day, Esther had told her to go and keep Gail, Samuel's wife, company, or at least provide reinforcements. Aaron had instantly offered, provided Isaiah approved, to drive her over and lend her *breider* a hand.

She'd sat as far away as possible on the silent ride over. Aaron wanted to speak, but what could he say beyond what was said last night? Repeating it wouldn't make a difference. Still, he took satisfaction that she was here. So was he. Regrettably, so was the Ohio fellow.

"At least it's something you can handle as there's no detail work involved. Just drive the nails in deep enough. I'll mud them over. I don't want to worry about my walls falling down." Aaron entered the room to see Samuel holding a sheet of drywall while Gideon and Malachi efficiently hammered it into place.

"Says the man who spends more time looking at the rear end of a horse anymore than viewing a finely lathed table leg," Gideon retorted.

Aaron's gaze raked Levi, who didn't seem to be doing anything other than wearing a disdainful expression at the current conversation. Determining to separate himself from Miriam's beau—*her other beau*, he amended with gritted teeth—he grabbed another sheet of drywall from the stack and set it in place next to Samuel's. Malachi, Miriam's oldest *bruder*, looked up, nodded and seamlessly moved over to continue driving nails.

"Once in a while he must look at the whole horse instead of just the rear end, as I'm pretty happy with the gelding I bought from him." Well familiar with brotherly banter, Aaron stepped into the conversation to support the local horse trader.

Samuel clapped him on the shoulder before grabbing another sheet from the stack. "That's what I like to hear. A satisfied customer."

"That makes one," quipped Gideon.

Setting the drywall in place, Samuel glanced over at Levi. "Feel free to pitch in anytime."

With a sigh, the man bent to pick up a hammer and sauntered over to where they were working.

"I'm a bit surprised Miriam didn't follow you out here. She's a fine woodworker and knows her way around tools. It was a tough choice as to who'd be the better asset to bring north with me when I moved. Her or you two. Sometimes I wondered if I chose wisely," Malachi murmured around the nails in his mouth.

"She's in the kitchen where a woman should be. Taking care of the home and garden and *kinner.* Not doing men's work in a shop. With my guidance, she will stifle her impulsive nature to do so."

All sounds of hammering except Levi's own erratic ones paused at the man's sanctimonious words.

Bristling, Aaron took a step toward where Levi haphazardly pounded in a nail. Bearing a clenched fist and gritted teeth, he bit his tongue when he noted the looks directed at the man's bent head. Samuel and Gideon's own jaws were tightened. Malachi's expression was unreadable, but it didn't bode well for the Ohioan. His wife, Ruth, had managed her father's furniture business prior to Malachi purchasing it at the older man's passing. She was an exceptional woodworker, something her husband was quite content to acknowledge.

Samuel hiked his eyebrows as he glanced at his two *breider*. Ignoring Levi's remark, he responded to his *bruder*'s comment. "She's a pretty *gut* horsewoman as well." His voice easily carried over the resumed hammering. "Do you remember her idea to race the draft horses? I think she beat all three of us. Of course the fastest race was getting back to the barn before *Daed* returned and saw what we were doing." Retrieving a tool and a few screws, he set them down next to Levi. "They're slower and more expensive, but if you can't drive the nails deep and true, you'll need to use the screws."

"I remember that race." Gideon picked up the conversation. "She also thought up putting the rope out to swing over the pond. She always went farther than us. Maybe that was the point. I'm surprised it didn't snap on her. You had that pleasure, didn't you, Malachi?"

"Not one of my better moments. It was quite a ride, though."

"She devised the best wedding pranks. After seeing some she'd suggested before we moved up here, I'm glad she restrained herself at ours." Samuel grunted as he set two sawhorses in place.

Aaron suppressed a smile as held his sheet in place for the others to hammer. Even he was impressed at the brothers' recitation of Miriam's past deeds—although he could tell from Levi Peachy's darkening expression the other man was not. Which was probably the Schrocks' intention.

"A leopard doesn't change its spots." Samuel measured the distance to the corner.

"Can't imagine her any other way." Gideon stuffed another handful of nails into his carpentry apron.

"Wouldn't want her any other way," Malachi confirmed as he prepared to cut the drywall on the sawhorses to the length Samuel called out.

All hammering and sawing stopped when Gail stepped through the doorway. "You interested in breaking for a drink and cookies?"

Samuel smiled at his visibly expectant wife. "*Ja.* I could be talked into it."

"More of a challenge to talk you out of food." Smiling, she disappeared to return a moment later, carrying a tray loaded with a pitcher of lemonade and some glasses. Miriam was a step behind with a plate of cookies. Aaron couldn't suppress his grin when she sought him out first before blushing and looking toward Levi.

Miriam wanted to kick herself for immediately searching for Aaron when she'd entered the room. Forcing a smile, she shifted her attention to Levi. Her pleasant look instantly faded when he glowered at her in return. Narrowing her gaze, she swept it over her brothers' innocent expressions. She sighed. They'd been teasing him.

Once, she might've been offended, but after having been separated from them for a few years, she'd missed them. And their teasing. Besides—she pressed her lips together at Levi's disgruntled expression—she wanted someone who could hold his own with her family. Someone they respected enough that any mutual badgering was good-natured. She watched from the corner of her eye as Samuel clapped Aaron on the shoulder. Even Gideon was joking with him—Gideon, who in support of his best friend, Ben Raber, had been reserved around Aaron when he'd initially returned. A reservation she'd cheered, as she'd more than felt the same way. And now…

Now she was trying to think of a way to remedy a situation where she didn't want the man she thought she'd wanted and *did* want the man she thought she didn't.

Now she had to mollify the visiting Levi out of his petulant mood when all she wanted to do was join in the playful banter with her brothers and sisters-in-law. Banter Aaron was easily included in.

So she did for a moment, while Levi sent her quelling looks Miriam refused to let quell her. Finally he sent her one she could no longer ignore. He tipped his head toward the door. With a sigh, she turned to follow him outside the unfinished room.

"Before you go, I'll take another one of those." She stopped at Aaron's request. Although his eyes were wary, reaching for the remaining cookie, he smiled. The sight of it flowed over Miriam like a warm bath after a frigid outing.

She couldn't do it. She couldn't go back to Ohio when…her heart was here. She'd thought she could when Levi had arrived yesterday afternoon and she'd joined him in a side room away from Esther and the children.

He'd reminded her why she'd initially thought he'd be a good match for her. Reminded her that she'd made poor judgments. Reminded her she couldn't be trusted not to make them again without his guidance.

But now, when the prospect of a life with Aaron was like an awakening spring and one with Levi a bitter winter, there wasn't a question of which one she longed for. *Ja*, Aaron had made mistakes. So had she. But Aaron said he wasn't going back. He was so many other wonderful things beyond the mistakes he'd made in his past. Surely it wasn't foolish to trust such a man with her heart?

Levi deserved to know her decision first. He was here because of an understanding she'd allowed. Had even encouraged.

Miriam trailed after his stiff shoulders into the kitchen. The resolution might hasten his trip back to Ohio, which would make most all involved happy, including reluctant host Gideon. But it didn't matter what her *bruder* thought of Levi anymore. He'd be an old acquaintance from Ohio and not a prospective brother-in-law.

Setting the plate on the counter, she twisted her hands together and prepared to reset the course of her life.

Levi turned to her, his mouth tight with

displeasure. "I see the eyes you're making at him. You're making the same mistake you made with Tobias. The one you allowed to shame you in front of your family and the whole community."

Heat crept up Miriam's cheeks.

"You don't want to do that again. Especially with someone else who's been in a jail. *Ja.* I found out about that. Surely sinning and jail time isn't what you want to share with a husband?" He took a step toward her. She retreated one.

"You need someone to guide you, Miriam. To help you suppress the impulsive nature I've been hearing about all morning. You need to be a *gut* and respected woman of the community. Someone your *kinner* can look up to. You don't want to continue making these mistakes. He—" Levi tipped his head toward where the sounds of construction could be heard "—might even end up in prison like Tobias. Like the man you foolishly chose before.

"These people need to be judged, not ogled or admired. I deigned to walk out with you to help you, to guide your judgment. You've sinned terribly, but with my guidance, you can again achieve righteousness back home in our district."

The tips of Miriam's ears were burning. Levi might assume it was shame. But anger fueled her more than embarrassment. She didn't know what stories her brothers had told. Surely other sisters with older brothers had done foolish things to keep up or be noticed. She was beyond that. Just as she was beyond the mistake she'd made. She'd confessed it. To *Gott* and the church. *Gott* had forgiven her. Even if she still struggled to forgive herself.

What she felt for Aaron wasn't a mistake. True, what he'd done was wrong. But he'd learned from that. It was behind him now. It was time to trust him. It was time to trust herself.

She was opening her mouth to tell Levi that he could go home without her, as she was staying to make her life in Miller's Creek, when Gail entered the kitchen carrying the tray with dirty glasses and an empty pitcher. She stopped at the sight of them.

"Sorry," she murmured, quickly backing out.

Miriam reddened further. Her *bruder*'s house with numerous witnesses was not the place to have the discussion ending their relationship. Fabricating a smile, she took a deep breath. It wasn't enough. She took another one.

"I know you expected me to come back

with you. But as Esther said, she's not ready yet to have me go. Conscientious as you are—" her lip curled slightly "—you'll understand I can't leave when I haven't fulfilled my obligations. As I won't be returning with you and I know you have responsibilities at home, I understand if you need to leave sooner than you intended."

Levi's mouth opened and closed a few times like a fish that'd been yanked up on land. He nodded with a jerk. "Tell your *bruder* I won't be able to stay to help him, and tell your other *bruder* that I'm taking the rig. I need to gather my things and check the bus schedule." Grabbing his coat, he left, shutting the door behind him with a sharp click.

Gail cautiously entered the kitchen. "Is everything all right?"

Miriam worried her lower lip. "Actually, I think it will be now." With a murmured excuse, she slipped out of the kitchen. A few steps into the other room, she steepled her hands and pressed them to her mouth.

She felt lighter. As if a burden had been lifted instead of a beau exiting. Maybe they were one and the same. Levi's sanctimoniousness, his inclination to judge—had that influenced her? It wasn't the way she'd been before. She'd thought she should be like him to win his approval. After the experience with Tobias, she'd latched on to Levi's interest, thinking his righteousness was what she needed. If it had been, it wasn't what she needed now, or who she wanted to be. At least not his version of it. Right or wrong, she wanted to trust herself. She had before Tobias. Surely she could do so again.

She blew out a breath. The man she'd thought would be so *gut* for her was not. And the one she knew would be so wrong for her... Maybe her judgment was in question. But not *Gott*'s. He'd sent her up here for a reason. She'd thought it was to take care of babies, but maybe it was to truly find her special someone.

Levi deserved to know first. She'd tell him they were no longer a betrothed couple the same way he'd confirmed they were— through the mail. And then she'd tell Aaron how she felt about him.

A grin spread over her face. For a man who always thought he knew what she was thinking, he was in for a surprise.

# Chapter Fifteen

The now empty milk cans rattled in the back of the wagon as Aaron drove the Percherons away from the cheese factory dock. As they passed the parking lot, he glanced over with a frown. He hadn't gotten a good glimpse of it when he'd pulled in, but there'd been a tail end of a car, tucked among the others in the store's parking lot, that'd caused icy fingers to walk up his spine.

His lips compressed. It was still there. Keeping an eye on it, he pulled out onto the road. He'd hoped to keep to the farm and out of Blake's reach. But he could hardly tell his boss he didn't want to make the milk delivery today, particularly after the man had given him the day off yesterday to help the Schrocks.

The Percherons' shoes rang on the blacktop. The sound, normally comforting, wasn't today when the back of his neck was twitching. It seemed to say *get home, get home, get home*. What a change from a year ago. Then, he couldn't wait to sneak off from home. Now, just the thought of the illegal work he'd done, the work he was being pressured to return to, made his stomach turn. Now, as the cadence suggested, he just wanted to make his home here, to stay in the community.

Lifting his hat, he ran his hand through his hair. Leaving, like he'd done before, might be one of the things synonymous with telling Blake no. His stomach churned further. He had to figure something out, because he'd promised Miriam he wasn't going back.

As he'd told her, he'd always been interested in anything with motors. Upon finishing school after eighth grade, he'd worked for his *daed* on the farm until his younger *breider* were old enough to finish and help. He'd bought a car at sixteen, one he'd happily tinkered on whether it needed it or not. At seventeen, his father finally gave in to his badgering and reluctantly let him work at an *Englisch* small engine shop. Aaron had quietly moved from there to an automotive repair shop, where he'd worked for some time without his father knowing.

*Ja*, he'd lied. It had troubled him some

then. It troubled him a lot more now. Had he ever asked for forgiveness from his *daed* for the deceit? *Nee.* His shoulders sagged under the guilt. He'd been furious back then when his *daed* found out about the job, went to the shop and told the owner Aaron couldn't work there anymore.

At the time, he'd been attending a lot of parties outside the Amish community. He'd grumbled at one about the situation in Blake's presence. After Aaron's passionate affirmative that he liked and knew cars, Blake had said he had a job for him, a job with all the car work Aaron could ever want. He'd started immediately. Initially, the job had entailed just stripping vehicles, but when Blake discovered he was adept at motor work, he was allowed to do that as well.

He hadn't asked questions about the cars' sources or parts' destinations, although he'd suspected. He'd started the job with defiance and passion. When it migrated to just passion, he'd started asking. He was flatly told he didn't need to know.

Now, he felt like a fool and the criminal he was for chopping stolen cars in the building adjacent to the scrap yard. Some had been local, but frequently they'd been lifted from the greater Madison area and brought up to the shop. There, a few were kept intact and moved to Milwaukee where they were used for street racing or, depending on their value, transported to the East Coast to ship out of the country. But primarily, the cars were stripped within a few hours of arriving, as it was a lot harder for authorities to trace parts rather than whole cars.

Aaron had learned, based on the model of the car, where to find and disable tracking devices. He'd learned to find and grind the VIN numbers hidden inside a vehicle. Whereas some folks thought vehicle identification numbers were only on the windshields or doors, manufacturers put them all over a car. He'd seen enough vehicles go by to know which ones were most frequently stolen.

When they didn't bring the whole vehicle into the shop to chop, Blake's gang brought in catalytic converters to ship out. If a vehicle was parked in a dark or isolated location, the valuable part containing trace amounts of precious metals could be quickly removed.

Once he'd known more, he'd wanted out, as had a coworker. One day, the guy was gone. While working underneath a car the day after the man's disappearance, Aaron had ominously overheard that his previous coworker would no longer be an issue. He'd immediately stopped any hinting that he also wanted to leave.

Instead, he'd worked out a plan and just took off. Left everyone. Family. Rachel. Friends. It'd been for the best at the time. He didn't know how he would've gotten out otherwise. Aaron scowled. He still wasn't out. Yet.

Keeping a low profile in Madison, he'd gone to school and gotten a part-time job. Anonymously, he'd sent money he'd saved while doing his illicit work—whatever he didn't need for his current livelihood—to support Bishop Weaver's medical bills when the man was hospitalized after a heart attack. As Amish didn't carry health insurance, the district paid any bills an individual member couldn't. It was the first time Aaron had contributed to the practice. Missing his community, it'd made him feel satisfied to be able to help in that way. Now the thought made him smile. If the bishop knew where Aaron's portion of the money had come from, it'd probably give him another heart attack.

When he'd returned home, his folks had welcomed him back like the prodigal son. The fatted calf was spared, but a couple of chickens hadn't been so fortunate. Although grateful, it had embarrassed him after what he'd put them through. People of the community—well, some at least, such as his folks, Isaiah, Ben and Rachel, the Schrocks—believed in him now. Aaron gnawed on the inside of his cheek. He couldn't blow that again. And Miriam?

He rubbed a hand over his mouth. He wanted to build a life with her. Have a family with Miriam Schrock.

He waited for the hesitancy, the uncertainty, the reluctance he'd felt when he'd thought about marrying Rachel. It wasn't there. What *was* there was excitement. Peace. Yearning. A smile on his face, a gladness in his heart and a longing in his arms.

Levi Peachy had gone home today. The Ohioan had returned to Ohio. Aaron didn't know what that meant, but the man was gone and he and Miriam were here. And he was going to make the most of that.

A flash reflected in the side mirror. Aaron glanced behind him. His smile faded. Eyes narrowed, he watched the car following slowly in his wake. Jaw tight, he looked around. The only things in view were the roof of the cheese factory shrinking with the distance, the pristine snow-covered fields, drifted ditches and—other than the tracking car—the empty road.

It was rare to see him without his posse, but as always, Blake had timed his ambush well.

Aaron drew in a deep breath and flexed his fingers on the leather lines. He wasn't anxious. Just...resolved. Blake would bide his time. The man was good at mind games and intimidation. There wouldn't be roaring engines. He was trying to psych him out by trailing him.

Well, Aaron wasn't going to play that game today. Or ever again. He would tell him he wasn't coming back.

The Percherons bobbed their heads in confusion as Aaron drew them to a gentle halt. Leaning back in the seat, he let the lines lie loose in his hands as he waited. His eyes stayed on the flickering ears of the draft team in front of him. His ears were tuned to the quiet rumble of the engine behind. When the wagon had halted, the car had stopped a short distance back. In the relative stillness, one of the geldings stomped his bucket-sized hoof.

The pitch of the motor changed. Aaron bit his lip. A glance back revealed the grill and gleaming dark hood of the car as it swerved out from behind the wagon to draw alongside him. Passing slowly, it turned in to a field entrance just beyond the waiting team and wheeled around to head back in Aaron's direction.

Tension vibrated through him as Blake pulled alongside the wagon. The dark-haired *Englischer* rolled down his window and leaned his arm on the door.

"Raber. I'm getting tired of tracking you down."

"I'll save you the trouble then. Don't. Because I'm not coming back."

The man smirked. "You don't quit on me. No one quits on me. Especially not some country rube."

"You think that's going to insult me?" Aaron shook his head. "I've been stared at and whispered about by folks like you a good share of my life."

Blake studied him with hooded eyes. "I have to admit, you're not what I expected. As far as cars go, you're actually pretty savvy." He flicked a glance to the waiting Percherons. "Surprising for someone more comfortable around manure than motors." The smirk disappeared as he returned his penetrating gaze to Aaron. Aaron had encountered black rat snakes that had more benevolence in their eyes.

"Remember Raber, you wanted in on this. You were practically tripping over yourself for a chance to work on the cars. You were so happy to do it that I almost let you do it for free. But I run a business. Everyone's more willing when there's a little green involved. And you made out pretty well on that end, too."

Aaron's stomach clenched at the accurate dart. His throat was as stiff as his face as he forced a swallow. "*Ja*, well, I was a fool. But that doesn't mean I have to remain one."

Blake's gaze never left him. Aaron stared back at the man, refusing to feel pinned like some captured insect on a board.

"I think you mean that." Blake pursed his lips. "That's too bad." He glanced over the wagon again. "Obviously money and the chance to work on cars aren't your motivators anymore." His eyes narrowed into mere slits as he scrutinized Aaron's carefully blank face. "I wonder what is…"

Aaron's breath grew shallow. *I can handle whatever he throws at me. I don't know what happened to my old coworker, but if I disappear, there'll be a number of folks who'll miss me this time, who'll ask questions and maybe come looking. Especially if I let them know I'm not planning on leaving. And if I have to leave, I'll let them know why. I'll let them know what they mean to me.* Miriam's animated features popped into his mind. *I was hoping for more time—perhaps a lifetime—*

*with her, but I've dragged her far enough into this. If I have to give her up for penance because of what I've been involved in*—his chest deflated as if every breath he'd ever taken had left him—*I will.*

A slow, sly smile crept across Blake's face. Even in the cold morning, sweat beaded on Aaron's forehead at the sight.

"I know what it is. The leverage to get you motivated again. It's the blonde."

The blood drained from Aaron's face. His mouth sagged open before he snapped it shut with a click of teeth. Bile coated the back of his throat.

"That's what I thought. Hmm. I always knew she was interesting. Now I know she's more than that. She's the key to you."

Aaron half rose from the seat of the wagon with fisted hands. "Keep away from her," he bit out through gritted teeth.

"Depends on you."

Sinking back down, Aaron's jaw remained clenched. He knew Blake. His previous boss always had an angle, usually one that applied painful pressure. Even knowing what to expect, he stiffened further at the man's drawl.

"*If* you come back to work. If not…" The man spread his hands as if things were out of his control. "She better stay in the barn or the house of that little dairy farm you both work on. Otherwise Blondie might find herself having a rough time. Oh, and don't think of leaving the area again, because that won't change the situation for her."

Aaron closed his eyes. Blood pulsed in the individual tips of his fingers as they dug into his thighs. He didn't care what Blake's gang did to him. He deserved it for his foolishness. He always knew this was a possibility if he came back—that he'd end up a victim of the gang or imprisoned due to the law. If he tried to report the gang, what proof did he have anymore? He knew from experience how quickly they could make the scrap yard, if that's even where they worked anymore, look like it was the business it advertised. He was trapped.

He couldn't, he wouldn't, let anything happen to Miriam.

Opening his eyes, he glared at the man watching with a self-satisfied smile. "If you touch one hair on her head…" Aaron didn't recognize the low growl of his own voice. His community, the teaching of his faith, had always been against violence of any kind. But that didn't stop the impotent anger surging through him at the threat to the woman he loved.

"Tsk, tsk, Raber." Blake shook his head mockingly. "I thought you people were pacifists." The mockery disintegrated from his face as Aaron started down from the wagon. "Whatever happens to her is up to you." When Aaron grimaced and paused, he had his response. "You know where the shop is. You'll hear as to when you're expected. And if you don't show, you know who we'll go looking for."

He shifted the car into gear. Instead of peeling out, it smoothly pulled away. It didn't matter. It still left scorch marks. They just weren't visible.

Aaron didn't remember getting the Percherons moving again. He couldn't feel his hands. They were numb. Not from cold, but from fear.

When Blake's car was out of sight, he pulled the team to the side of the road. Lurching down from the wagon, he staggered to the ditch and was sick. Hands on his hips, he gulped down deep breaths of the cold air.

He had no choice.

His empty stomach continued to churn. It was Miriam's physical safety, or his emotional and spiritual well-being. His…dreams. There was no choice at all. He'd do whatever was necessary to protect Miriam, even though there'd be no future with her. And his future... It was worse off than before. Now, if he disappeared, it'd be due to Blake's choice—and it would mean Aaron's demise. The only other path of departure traveled through jail. With shaky legs, he climbed back into the wagon.

From its perch, Aaron looked across the landscape of fields blanketed by pristine snow. He thought—he'd hoped—he'd be in position to be like that. Maybe not pristine, but clean again. Respectable. To others and to himself. He wanted to build up, not tear down anymore like the cars he'd soon be chopping, or his hopes, which were now disintegrating.

With a sigh, he picked up the lines. He didn't know which he dreaded more—the message he'd heard from Blake, or the one he had to share with Miriam.

Miriam watched the kitchen door close behind Aaron. He'd been quiet at supper. Even the *kinner*, whom he always had smiles for, couldn't change his somber mood. He didn't even stay to interact with them as usual this evening. In fact, all the Zooks were staring at the closed door he'd disappeared behind. She caught Isaiah's eye. Frowning, he headed for his chair, picked up the newspaper and lifted it as a barrier. Frowning too at Aaron's action, she gathered the dishes from the table.

With the older Zook girls' help, the kitchen was soon in order for the evening. The girls departed the kitchen as Esther entered. Wiping her hands on a dish towel, Miriam glanced again toward the door.

"Why don't you go see?" The woman tipped her head toward where Aaron had exited.

It was all the encouragement Miriam needed. Besides, she wanted to talk with him. She'd penned a letter to Levi, ending their relationship. It was in her room, waiting for tomorrow's mail. Just having written it felt like it completed her obligation to the man she'd once thought she'd wanted. Now she was excited to commit to the one she actually did. Hastily, she put on her coat and headed out the door.

Aaron looked up as she entered the tack room. Instead of the greeting she'd anticipated, he pressed his lips into a thin line and returned his attention to the harness he was cleaning. Furrowing her brow, Miriam strolled over to stroke a hand down the smooth surface of one of the horse collars.

"There's a lot to keep clean."

He grunted. "*Ja*. Well, sometimes it's impossible to do so, even with *gut* intentions."

She waited for him to look up. He didn't. Miriam wrinkled her nose. The man made a habit of making things difficult. She wanted to be subtle, to tease, to flirt, to ease into this important conversation, but that wasn't looking like an option.

She propped her hands on her hips. "I was hoping for a chance to talk with you alone. There's something I want to tell you."

He still didn't look up. Just mumbled, "There's something I need to tell you as well."

Although she was bursting with her news, his, whatever it was, obviously needed to come off his chest. She didn't want it to taint what she was going to share. She'd let him go first and then lift his mood with hers.

"All right. I'm listening."

Aaron finally looked up. Miriam felt an uneasy ripple move up her spine when his hand tightened around the brush in his hand until his knuckles turned white. His strong throat bobbed in a hard swallow.

"I'm going back to work for Blake."

"What?" She cocked her head. She couldn't have heard him right.

His chest rose and fell in a prolonged sigh. "I'm going back to work for Blake."

He might as well have slapped her.

"But...but why? It's illegal. You...you promised."

Flinging the brush to the bench before him, he pushed to his feet and turned away. "My promises don't mean anything. Don't you recall? I broke an engagement."

Her lips felt numb. "That one turned out for the best."

He spun to face her. "Things don't always turn out for the best. But in this case, the best for me is to go back to work for him." His jaw firmed. He crossed his arms over his chest. "I've missed working on cars like I used to."

"You're lying." A tear leaked from the corner of her eye. She dashed it away with shaking fingers.

"I told you I was a liar. What are you going to do?" He gestured toward the harness collars from which curved pieces of iron jutted. "Hit me with the hames this time?"

"If I thought it would do any good, I would."

Aaron looked away again. He couldn't face her eyes, shimmering with tears. Eyes that said he was betraying her. How could that be? The only way he could betray her was if she'd believed in him. Had she?

"Just because it's best for you, doesn't mean it is for others. Think of them for once."

*I am. I am thinking of others. I'm returning to that work to keep you safe. I'd rather risk everything than have you hurt. I love you.* His breathing shallowed at the wild possibility that popped into his head.

"Maybe…maybe they can work out best for the both of us."

"What do you mean?" She crossed her arms over her chest.

"Come with me. We'll go down to Madison. Or Milwaukee even. I know I can get a job working on cars." For the first time since he'd seen Blake on the road, hope began to bubble through him.

Miriam blinked rapidly. Her mouth sagged. The tears trickling down her cheeks slowed. She was going to agree. It was a *wunderbar* idea. He and Miriam. They could make it. Leaving for the *Englisch* wouldn't be so bleak with her by his side.

Then her mouth began to tremble. Her beautiful blue eyes were again awash with tears.

"I can't. I've been baptized. If I leave, I'll be shunned. I won't be able to see my family again. My *mamm* or *daed*. Or my siblings. I want to see their families grow up. I want to have a family that will grow up with theirs. I… I can't leave."

Aaron sagged against the wall of the tack room, knocking the big draft horse bridles askew. Just like that, all energy left him. For a moment, he'd thought—he'd hoped—that he'd be enough. Seemed the only one he was enough for was Blake. He couldn't tell Miriam why he was doing it. She'd try to talk him out of it. She didn't know Blake. Let her think the worst of him. She'd done it before. Her path back in that direction would be easily traveled. Though it made him ill to have her think poorly of him, it would devastate him if she was hurt in any way because of him.

"I'm going back to Ohio." Her voice quavered. "I can't stay here and see you do what you're doing to yourself. I can't be here and watch you go to jail again. Or from there to prison. Once was enough. Because this time, I'm afraid you'll stay there."

She turned and went out. At the muffled bang of the outer barn door, Aaron slid to the floor. What difference did it make if he went to prison? With Blake's hold over him, he might as well already be there.

# Chapter Sixteen

Miriam looked out over the night-shrouded fields as she tucked the buggy blanket more tightly about her hips. Thankfully, Levi had left a bus schedule at Gideon's place. One was leaving tonight for Ohio. She would be on it. Levi's unsent letter was packed with the rest of her things—leaving the opportunity to resume that relationship once she reached home? Maybe he'd been right. Aaron had proven she was a fool to trust herself.

She sniffed.

Gideon glanced over at her. "Are you crying because you're going, or because you're not going fast enough?"

"What does that mean?" Miriam wiped her mitten under her nose. Trust her brother to be insensitive. He'd only wanted her in Wisconsin to cook and keep house for him. Of course, that hadn't worked out, as she'd only stayed a few sporadic days with him, and stayed at others' homes for her job the rest of the time. But he hadn't seemed to mind. At least he hadn't said anything.

"It means, if you're crying because you're not going fast enough, then it's probably the right choice to be returning to Ohio."

"Of course it's the right thing to do. It's what I planned all along. What I need to do. I just feel bad for leaving Esther so abruptly." Returning to the house last night after Aaron's devastating news, Miriam had mumbled some garbled reason as to why she had to go back to Ohio as soon as possible. To her relief, after a piercing look at her, Esther had accepted her flimsy excuse, assuring Miriam they'd be fine.

Gideon ignored her vehement protest. "But if you're crying because you're going, then maybe you need to rethink your decision."

Miriam wanted to refute his comment. Instead, she furrowed her brow at her brother's profile. "What do you know of it? Of my older brothers, you're the only one who's still single."

"Maybe that makes me the expert."

His grin faded as he shifted to face her. "I didn't suggest you come up here just so I didn't have to cook. I know how to open a can and fry an egg, and I receive more than a dish or two of unsolicited home-cooked food."

"No accounting for taste I guess." Although her remark was flippant, Miriam considered her brother with narrowed eyes. Even through a sister's skeptical lens she could see many qualities that would prompt the single women of Miller's Creek to pursue her *bruder*.

"Theirs or mine? Some of them think they're better cooks than they are."

"Then why did you?"

"Accept the meals? They were free and offered and something I didn't have to fix myself."

"*Nee.* Suggest I come up."

He slowed down to turn a corner. When Miriam recognized the road containing the restaurant that housed the bus stop, heartache weighed on her shoulders as if heavy hands were pushing her into the seat. She firmed her lips to keep them from trembling.

"*Mamm* was worried about you."

Blinking the sting of threatening tears from the back of her eyes, Miriam shook her head. "*Mamm* was worried about me? She never said. You're making that up."

"She was worried you were going to punish yourself for a lifetime for a little mistake."

"A little mistake! I went to jail! I embarrassed my family and myself. I've never felt so horrible in my life. It wasn't a *little* mistake."

"Marrying the wrong man would be a bigger one. Are you really planning to marry Levi Peachy?"

Miriam opened her mouth, but nothing came out. Clearing her throat, she tried again.

"Here's where you're supposed to say that Levi isn't the wrong man. Just in case you missed your cue. The fact that you did tells me something. And it should tell you something, too."

This time she couldn't keep the tears from welling into her eyes. "I should marry Levi," she murmured.

"I still don't hear a *want*. Levi is… *Ach*, he's not the sort of man I envisioned for you, which sounds *narrish*, as I've not envisioned a woman for myself. But it's not crazy for a *bruder* to want his sister to be happy. And I don't think he'll make you happy. You don't seem to…love him. Why do you need to marry him?" Gideon's eyes rounded. He looked uncomfortable. "You're not…expecting a *boppeli*, are you?"

*"Nee."* Miriam quickly put the possibility to rest. The thought of having a family with

Levi made her curl her lip. Thinking further about it, it curled her stomach as well. Did she really want Levi to help raise her children? To subject them to his sanctimonious attitude? Or would she rather have them grow up with a father more like… Aaron? Who would tease them and play with them and care for them unconditionally?

Marrying Levi would be a way to punish herself for her misdeed. A method of penance. Of protection to deter further impulsiveness. Staid Levi would never be impulsive. She couldn't imagine laughing with him. Miriam worried her lower lip. It would be nice to laugh with a spouse. Unbidden, the memory of a kitten climbing from Aaron's shoulder to the top of his head while the surrounding children giggled popped into Miriam's head. Even now, the incident made her smile.

The neon lights of the restaurant were in view. The place looked quiet this time of a winter evening. Miriam pulled the blanket closer. She wished she could take it with her. It would be a long, cold ride to Ohio.

"Got a few minutes before the bus arrives. Time enough to think about whether you want me to turn around and take you back home." Gideon's words were subdued as he guided the horse to a rail set on the back fringe of the parking lot.

Although Miriam loved her family in Ohio, Wisconsin already felt like home. But she couldn't be with a man who'd willingly break the law. Could she stay in the area, knowing what he was doing and not expose him? Could she expose him when she was very much afraid she...loved him?

She sighed. "I need to get my suitcase. The bus will be here soon. I can wait in the restaurant if you want to head back."

Gideon echoed her sigh. "I'll wait with you. I might not say it much, but I do like having you around. And if you want to come back to see me, or anyone else, I'm sure we'd be happy to tolerate your company."

Miriam pressed her hand against her mouth, glad the sound that escaped came out as a hiccup instead of the stifled sob it was. She intentionally misconstrued whom he might be talking about. "I liked being around Malachi and Samuel and their growing families. And I'll certainly be back to attend your wedding, should you ever get around to having one."

"For sure and certain, if you're waiting for that, you won't be back for a while." He smiled wryly. "Everyone but me seems in such a hurry to get married." He reached for her suitcase, nestled behind the seat. Pushing the door open, he turned back, the smile gone from his face. "Marriage is for life, Miriam. Make sure when you choose that life, you choose it for the right reasons."

Miriam climbed down from the buggy. Her feet were as heavy as her heart at her pending departure. "I have my reasons for leaving."

With drooped shoulders, she started across the parking lot. At the glare of bright headlights turning into the restaurant's entrance, she lifted her hand to shield her eyes. One car, then another, then a third drove in. Miriam froze. The cars crossed the parking lot, pulling around her and Gideon in a U-shape that blocked their path to the restaurant. The window of the middle car rolled down to reveal a dark-haired man. His eyes raked over her before he smirked.

"Hello, Blondie."

He should've checked the bus schedule. She could be already gone. He'd raced over to Gideon's place, hoping to stop her as soon as Esther told him Miriam was returning to Ohio. Within seconds of discovering the empty house, he was on the road again.

She was going back to Levi. Aaron scowled.

Levi wasn't right for her. Levi didn't understand her. He wouldn't appreciate her nimble mind, sarcastic tongue and caring nature. She'd be stifled by him. Sanctimonious Levi didn't deserve her. Neither did he, but... Aaron flopped back against the buggy seat.

He loved her. And he couldn't let her leave without telling her so. Hunching forward again as if he were a jockey instead of a driver, he urged the Standardbred faster.

She might not listen. It might not make a difference. But he had to tell her. *If* she hadn't already left. Up ahead, he saw headlights on the highway leading into town. Samuel Schrock had said the gelding had speed. Aaron needed all it had. It still wouldn't exceed the racing of his heart.

Minutes later he swept around the corner to the street where neon lights advertised Miller's Creek's fast food eatery, which housed the bus stop. Beyond the rapid cadence of hoofbeats he could hear the rumble of high performance engines. Aaron's breath caught. Automatically, he pressed his right foot down in an effort to go faster as if he, too, were in a car. The action gained him nothing beyond grinding pebbles into the floorboard of his buggy.

A cold breeze rushed in when he jerked the buggy door open. A trio of cars was semi-circled in the dimly lit parking lot. Inside their perimeter was a smaller ring of dark figures. A solitary Amish buggy parked at the lot's back edge. The horse's head was raised and cocked toward the rumbling cars.

Aaron wheeled his horse into the entrance. The gelding's hooves skidded on the snow-packed drive. As the rig rushed past the crowd, between the idling cars Aaron glimpsed a figure sprawled on the ground. An Amish woman was silhouetted where she knelt beside the prone man. Aaron was out the door even as the gelding drew next to the other rig. Fists and jaw clenched, stomach weighted with lead, he strode to the gathering. The circle parted to reveal Gideon still on the ground. His hat lay a few feet away. Even in the erratic street and car lighting, it was obvious one eye was swelling. Blood dripped from his nose and the corner of his mouth.

Miriam's hand was on her brother's shoulder. She glanced toward Aaron, her face white as milk. From a distance, she appeared unhurt. He drew his first real breath since turning the corner onto the street. His gaze swept the perimeter of the circle until he spied Blake. His old boss was the only one still sitting in a car, a few feet beyond where Miriam knelt. Heart pounding, Aaron stalked over.

Upon closer inspection, Miriam's bonnet hung by its ties from her neck. Her *kapp* was askew. Her pale face was unmarked, though. The same couldn't be said of Gideon. He looked worse up close. Quickly scanning the surrounding men, Aaron noted the abraded and bloody knuckles of the one who stood behind Miriam.

Slapping his hands on the top of the car, Aaron glared down at his boss. "This wasn't part of it. You said you wouldn't bother her if I came back."

"I said I wouldn't touch *her*. I didn't say anything about not touching anyone else. Knowing how you feel about her, I thought I was doing you a favor, Raber," the man drawled. "She looked like she was out with someone else. How was I to know it was her brother?" His tone hardened. "Besides, I wanted you to remember who was in charge. You still seemed reluctant. I wanted to make sure I got action out of you."

There was a flicker of movement in the corner of Aaron's eye. "I'll give you some action," he bit out. Whirling, he swung at the man who gripped Miriam's arm and was dragging her to her feet, the one obviously responsible for Gideon's bruised and battered face.

His fist connected with a thud. The impact

stung his hand, and also his heart when he caught Miriam's horrified expression. The man—apparently not expecting to be struck by an Amish man—staggered, letting go of Miriam. She scrambled back over to where Gideon was sprawled on the snow-packed asphalt.

His will to fight immediately extinguished, Aaron's arms dropped to his sides. His aggression had defeated the teaching of his district. Refuted the principles of the community he was striving to return to. The hands that eagerly restrained his arms weren't needed. Aaron ached even before a punch to his midsection drove all the air from his body. Hard knuckles slammed his lips against his teeth and flung his head back. His mouth filled with the taste of copper as he doubled over.

Breathing raggedly, Aaron tried not to be sick on the parking lot. Booted feet converged on him. He glanced past the dark-clad legs to where Miriam crouched beside Gideon. Rough hands on his shoulders pulled him erect. He spit out a mouthful of blood, somewhat gratified to see one of those closing in jump back to avoid it. Aaron grimaced. For sure and certain, Gideon looked worse, but at least he hadn't betrayed everything he'd been raised to believe. As Aaron wasn't yet baptized into the church, he wouldn't be shunned for his actions. The knowledge was no comfort. Even though he wouldn't be shunned, for some in the community, this action might be the final straw against him.

Running his tongue over the ragged edges inside his lips, he snuck another look at the pair now on the outside of the ring of grim faces. He couldn't let Blake hurt others. At least now the blows would be on the one who deserved them.

Over the next few moments, Aaron could only be glad that farm work built strong bodies. He couldn't and wouldn't hit back, but, as he tightened his muscles, he hoped the punching hands felt the impacts as well. He heard Miriam's gasp over his own grunt as another blow fell.

The pounding paused for a second. The crisp, clear night carried the faint sound of a siren. Had someone from the restaurant called the cops?

Blake revved the motor of his car. Apparently it was a signal, because everyone piled into their vehicles.

At his sudden release, Aaron staggered. Holding his midsection, he choked on the exhaust as Blake pulled close to where he swayed. "Do we understand each other, Raber?" As

Aaron stared back, the dark-haired man continued. "Monday night. You know where. Otherwise, you know what will happen."

The sound of sirens was louder. Blue-and-red lights flickered in the distance.

The trio of cars roared out the drive and skidded into the street. Aaron stumbled to where Miriam was helping Gideon sit up. Extending a hand, he was relieved when, although Gideon considered it for a moment, he finally grasped it. Aaron's groans echoed Gideon's as he helped the man to his feet. Miriam rose as well, her face tight with anxiety.

Pressing his hand to his side, Gideon bent at the waist. As much as he was hurting, Aaron would rather have incurred Miriam's brother's injuries as well instead of having Gideon suffer them. This was all his fault.

"Do you need a doctor?" he mumbled through painful lips.

*"Nee."* Blowing out a slow breath, Gideon straightened. "I've been kicked by a few horses before. Those felt worse."

An SUV, with SHERIFF emblazoned on the side, rolled to a stop beside them. The blue-and-red flashing lights reflected on the side of the silver bus that pulled in behind it.

With the hiss of brakes, the bus pulled up to the restaurant.

A trim young man exited the SUV to approach them. Even through swelling eyes, Aaron recognized Deputy Stone from the jail. The man's encompassing gaze swept the three of them. "Are you all right?"

Aaron shared a glance with Gideon. "Just a...disagreement with some...unhappy customers. They said the fries were cold. We said they tasted fine to us."

The deputy's mouth twitched. "Must've been very unhappy. I thought you guys didn't fight?"

Gideon raised his hand. "I didn't."

"It seemed like a *gut* idea before it didn't." Aaron glanced at Miriam. "In many ways."

Behind the deputy, the driver descended from the bus and lifted the luggage compartment. He looked around as if he was expecting someone before entering the restaurant.

Aaron glanced at the abandoned suitcase, lying on its side several yards away. With more apprehension than when confronted by Blake's henchmen, he searched Miriam's face. She was worrying her lip as she looked from Gideon to the silver bus.

Groaning, Gideon sagged against her. Aaron stepped forward. Gideon must've taken a turn for the worse. He'd seemed better just a moment ago. Was the adrenaline wearing off, making aches and pains howl within him as it was with Aaron?

Deputy Stone strode forward as well, his face grim. "Are you sure you don't want to go to the hospital?"

"I'll be fine." Gideon's mumble was barely discernible.

Miriam put Gideon's arm around her shoulder and helped him straighten. "I'll get my *bruder* home and take care of him."

Aaron almost sagged himself with relief at her words.

Gideon turned an eye, the one not swollen shut, on Aaron. "You might want to follow us home. Between the cold and the buggy's suspension, I'll be pretty stiff by the time I get there. Could be a challenge for Miriam to take care of both me and the horse."

"I can give you a ride out to your place," the deputy promptly offered.

"*Nee*, I think we can manage. Besides," Gideon's smile looked a little grotesque with his inflated mouth, "I want to keep my status as the only one of this group who hasn't ridden in a patrol car."

The officer furrowed his brow but didn't

pursue the comment. "Do you have a phone in case you determine you need some help?"

*"Ja."* Gideon nodded before wincing.

Although he shook his head, Deputy Stone picked up the suitcase and, following them to the buggies, helped them get settled in. The bus pulled out of the parking lot before they did. Aaron bid it good riddance as he followed Gideon's rig.

By the time he got to Gideon's place, Aaron had stiffened up enough that he wasn't sure if he could get down from his own buggy, much less help Gideon out of his. Groaning, he pushed himself off his seat and cautiously descended.

After helping Miriam get her *bruder* into the house, Aaron took care of the horse. Wanting to check on them again before he left, he limped back to the house. Gideon was in his chair. A bag of packed snow wrapped in a towel was propped against his face.

Aaron gingerly leaned against the wall as he studied him. What do you say to a man who gets beaten to a pulp because of you? "I'm so sorry about this. You're a paragon. I'll tell you what, I'll let you marry my sister."

*"Ach,* no need to punish a man for *gut* behavior." Gideon's eyes remained closed. His response was muffled by the cold pack.

No reciprocating jest was made that Aaron could marry Gideon's sister, the sister who even now wouldn't look at him. Aaron took a deep breath, grimacing at the pain the action generated in his chest. "I'm so sorry." He turned to the door. To his surprise and cautious joy, Miriam followed him to the porch.

Pulling the door shut, she crossed her arms over her chest. "Too bad the one who willfully breaks the rules isn't the one who gets into trouble."

Her attitude was no more than he deserved. Aaron hung his head. "You're right. This is my fault. My responsibility."

"I'd say the one responsible is your friend Blake."

Looking up in surprise that she didn't directly blame him, Aaron would've smiled if the action didn't hurt so much. "He's not my friend." He touched a finger to his abused mouth. "*Ja*, Blake's responsible. Although he wasn't the one who hit me. He doesn't do his own dirty work. Except for stealing the high-end cars. He gets a thrill out of that."

"Too bad he doesn't get caught with evidence like Tobias." She almost spat the name.

"*Ach*, that's one thing that'll never happen with Blake. He's too smart to be caught with evidence. Although he's at the shop when the cars come in, he doesn't strip them. Or at least he didn't." Aaron closed his eyes against the pressure of the swelling. "He had an office, though. He may have something in there." He grunted. Come Monday, he might have a chance to find out. Without proof, it was just Blake's word against his. And as Aaron had learned from his trip to jail, Blake was already skilled at manufacturing witnesses.

Lights flashed across them as a vehicle turned into the lane. Aaron tensed before he recognized the deputy's SUV. Miriam immediately slipped back inside the house. Hobbling down the steps, Aaron went to where the vehicle parked next to the front gate.

"Just checking to make sure you got home all right."

"*Ja.* So far." With slitted eyes, Aaron could see the man studying him through the open window.

"Good. Cold fries are serious business."

Aaron snorted. He could like this *Englisch* man. "There might've been a little more to it than that."

"Really? I guess that doesn't surprise me, considering I recognized the cars that sped out of the lot." Tapping fingers on the side of the vehicle, Deputy Stone scrutinized Aaron further. "We've been trying to pin something on Blake for some time. He seems quite interested in you. Care to share why?"

Aaron sighed. To dodge the situation he'd mired himself in, he'd tried flight and now fight. Neither had worked and had only made him and others suffer more. It was time—it was past time—to trust *Gott*. With soul-deep fatigue, he lifted a silent prayer. The officer waited quietly. Following a hard swallow, Aaron rasped, "We might have a little history. One I'd like to leave behind."

Deputy Stone nodded. "We might be able to help you out with that if you give us a hand."

## Chapter Seventeen

Miriam rested her forehead against the cow's warm flank as her hands squirted milk into the bucket, a task she'd done so many times she could do it with her eyes closed. The automatic action was soothing, something she could use right now.

Although she was back helping the Zooks during the day, she returned to Gideon's place in the evening, something she'd started doing to help him right after the incident two weeks ago and had continued after his speedy recovery. She hadn't caught more than a glimpse of Aaron in that time, although he still worked, on occasion, for the Zooks.

He was apparently spending more and more time at his *other* job. *You said you wouldn't bother her if I came back.* Her ears hadn't deceived her on the awful night. Aaron had gone back to work for Blake because the man had threatened her. *Knowing how you feel about her.* Unlike Tobias, who'd sought to pull her into his criminal activities, Aaron had returned to them to protect her. Miriam wanted to assure him that she didn't need his protection, but having watched Gideon's bruises fade from purple to a faint greenish-yellow, she wasn't sure. Still, the thought of Aaron doing illegal work for that man because of her made her sick.

While the community might not know of his illicit work, news he'd thrown a punch quickly made the rounds. Response in the district was mixed. A few thought even though he wasn't yet baptized, Aaron should be punished somehow for his action. Others concluded that the man had confessed his sin to one of the ministers and, having seen Aaron's bruised and battered face, thought he'd been punished enough.

If she went back to Ohio like she'd planned, removing herself as leverage, could Aaron quit? Would Blake pursue her there? She didn't want to leave. She hadn't been wrong to trust Aaron. She hadn't been wrong to trust her feelings for him. He was trapped in a past mistake he'd made. She'd made a mistake before, a painful one. But her mistake now would be losing him.

She loved him. She had from the moment he'd reluctantly, reverently, held his nephew in his arms in the company of his brother and the woman he'd previously wronged. He wasn't the same man he'd been then, just as she wasn't the same woman who'd originally come to Wisconsin. It'd taken her too long to recognize that.

With her forehead pressed against the cow and the sounds and smells of the milking parlor surrounding her, Miriam lifted a prayer. *Oh* Gott, *I know not how, but please help him.* When she leaned back, she felt the peace that'd been eluding her.

If Aaron was arrested for his activity because of her, she'd stay for him until he was released, whenever that was. Although traumatic, she'd proven to herself that she could face her fear. Having done it once, she could do it again. Miriam exhaled slowly. Now, if only she had the chance to tell Aaron that. She hadn't talked with him since that night when he'd spoken with the deputy outside Gideon's house and then disappeared.

When Isaiah had surprisingly asked her to stay tonight and help with the milking, she'd hoped to see him. But, heading to the barn with anticipation, her feet had slowed when she'd seen Aaron's rig was gone.

So where was he? There was one way to find out. Rising from the side of the cow, she retrieved the full bucket. As she passed where Isaiah was milking, she injected casualness in her voice. "Where's Aaron?"

Hands remaining busy, he looked up. "I was wondering when you'd ask. He has special work tonight. He and the sheriff's department are going to stop this Blake fellow."

Miriam dropped her bucket. Hitting the concrete with a bang, it remained upright but milk sloshed over the edges.

"*Ja.* He cleared his work with the authorities with Bishop Weaver before he proceeded. You weren't aware?" The dairyman smiled. "Even though our grapevine is rampant, I suppose we know when to be quiet as well."

Miriam felt as if she were the one who'd taken a blow to the stomach. Blake was dangerous. If he found out what Aaron was up to, he'd do more than beat him. But if the plan succeeded, Aaron would be free…

"How do you know all this?" she asked weakly.

Standing, Isaiah patted the back of the Holstein he'd been milking. "You can only spend so much time in a barn talking only to the cows."

Her heart pounding, Miriam retrieved the

bucket. As much as she was shaking, she was surprised she had any milk left in it by the time she reached the milk house. Setting it down, she sagged onto an empty milk can. *Oh* Gott, *I should've known You'd have a plan. I trust in Your will. But please let it include his safety. I know why You brought me to Wisconsin. To find my special someone. Please don't let me lose him now.*

Despite the coolness of the shop, sweat trickled down Aaron's back. He'd avoided looking at the light poles when he'd driven in, knowing what looked like electrical equipment on them were actually cameras. The man who ran the salvage yard, also knowing it was cover for the chop shop, had left for the day, leaving only Aaron and his coworker, a young *Englischer* who seemed more jumpy than Aaron was. Perhaps he would testify against Blake when this was over. Aaron could only hope so. He was ready for it to be over. All over. And tonight would determine whether it was.

It hadn't been difficult to act the broken-spirited man when he'd started back to work for Blake. After more than a week of watching him like a hawk, his boss seemed to have eased his suspicions and he'd started conversing in Aaron's presence about the business.

Aaron had told the authorities all he knew from when he'd worked at the shop before and what he'd learned since. Using the information, they'd set up bait cars—cars with audio, video, GPS, even disabling capability—in Portage, the largest town in the county. Some were trucks and cars commonly used for chopping, a few—where the big money was—were high-end vehicles stolen to ultimately ship out of the country under different VIN numbers. If they were to catch Blake in the act, it'd be with a luxury car which he personally lifted. An order for one such vehicle had come in. Blake was planning to steal it tonight. With word out there was one in Portage, he'd forgo the longer trip to Madison. Or so Aaron hoped.

He flinched when his newly obtained phone rang, indicating the shop's doors needed opening. With a ragged heartbeat, Aaron pressed the button that did so. A gleaming Porsche pulled into one of the bays, followed by a Honda Accord. Instead of re-pressing the button to close the doors once the cars were inside, Aaron strode to the far wall. As soon as Blake and the others exited the vehicles, authorities swept into the shop through various doors. At the cacophony of shouts and blur of activity, his breathing suspended. It could've so easily been him being handcuffed again, along with the others. Aaron's stomach clenched when Blake's hooded gaze met his as the man slowly lifted his arms away from his body at a deputy's directive.

Some moments later, Aaron folded his arms over his chest to conceal his still trembling hands as Deputy Stone approached him. "Did you get what you needed?"

"And then some. And your coworker wanted out. He's almost bursting to testify."

"Good. Because as we'd agreed, I won't." Aaron released a shuddering exhalation. "Are you finished with me then?" He couldn't believe it was finally over. The trouble he'd gotten himself into could finally be put behind him. And his future? It depended on Miriam. If she was set to return to Ohio, he'd follow her. Surely they needed someone there to work on motors, or even just to milk cows. In time, hopefully she'd accept that his days of breaking rules were over and learn to trust him.

Nodding, the deputy squinted at Aaron. "Your choice, but someone wants to talk with you." He tipped his head outside, to where

Blake stood handcuffed next to another officer.

His mouth dry, Aaron walked out to the pair.

"Raber. I should've known. Lately you'd been much too…submissive." Blake lazily rolled his shoulders against his restraints. "You were the only one who left, shall we say, without my permission. I took that personally. You see, I recognize a lot of me in you, Raber. That's why I kept pursuing you. You're a risk-taker. We both have a hunger."

"You're wrong." Aaron slowly shook his head. "I don't have an appetite for anything like what you do. Not anymore."

Blake raised an eyebrow. "You keeping Blondie? I know you care about her. You know," he sighed as he smiled ruefully, "if I'd had a girl like her, or a community like yours, I might've turned out differently. Guess we'll never know now."

Aaron watched silently as the officer directed Blake into the back of an SUV. He turned away. His knees suddenly felt so rubbery, he wondered if he'd be able to make it to his buggy.

Staggering the last few yards, he slumped against the wheel when he reached its support. He couldn't undo the past few years, but he could atone for them, and positively move forward. That was something Blake, for all his faults, had rightly understood. Aaron was grateful for his community. And if he had another chance with Miriam, he'd be more than grateful.

An hour later, when he drove up Gideon's lane, Aaron's hands were trembling almost as much as they had when the arrests were made at the chop shop. That shut the door on his past. This would hopefully open it to his future. Words had always come easily to him, but tonight, when it was so important, he didn't know what to say. Would she even listen to him? His gaze drifted over the snowy yard. Unlike the Zooks', with a houseful of children, it was pristine. An idea began to form.

Skirting the front porch, he went through the gate to the side yard where untouched snow glistened in the moonlit night. Leaping to leave several feet between his tracks, Aaron began stomping out an area. When the door slammed, he looked over to see Miriam sliding her arms into the sleeves of her coat as she exited the house. To his relief, she stayed on the step.

"What are you doing?" Her voice was curious. Receptive? He could only hope.

Finishing his outline, Aaron compacted the space inside it while his pulse galloped. From the middle of his handiwork, he turned to her. Surely the clear starry night held air, but none of it seemed to find its way into his lungs.

"It's my heart, Miriam. You can either trample it, or you can fill it."

From her perch on the step, she crossed her arms over her chest. The moments ticked by. Aaron began to feel a cold that had nothing to do with the temperature.

"Looks like another jail cell to me."

Aaron wanted to sink to the snow in defeat. How would he ever regain her trust?

He had to clear his voice twice before he could speak. "It's meant to keep you secure, rather than trap you."

She was going to say no. Rachel would've said yes if he'd asked her to marry him. He hadn't wanted to ask, had used his avoidance to do so as one of the many reasons he'd run. Now, the girl he wanted to ask, whom he couldn't imagine living without, would always consider him a lawbreaker. Would she ever forgive him for his past mistakes? He rubbed a hand over the back of his neck. "I know what you're thinking."

"I doubt it." Miriam jumped from the step into the untouched snow. With furrowed brow, Aaron watched her shuffle a short path, occasionally backtracking. Much as he willed it, she wouldn't look at him. Finally, he left his perplexed attention on her feet. What was she doing?

He'd never felt less like playing a game. "Why can't you just say it? You've never been shy about speaking your mind before."

Shaking her head, she hopped over a clear patch of snow to start another path. She hopped again to start a new one. And again. Letters? What was she spelling? Looking back over the markings, he braced himself for a message of GO AWAY, GET LOST or FORGET IT.

When he saw the words she'd traced, he went back and read them again. And a third time. He ran over to where she was finishing the last letter.

"You're going to mess them up. You'll forget what it says."

Plucking her out of her shuffled path, Aaron pulled her into his arms. With her safely tucked there, he fell back into the I LOVE YOU that was set into the snow.

"Never. I'll never forget them. They're written on my heart."

"No they're not. Your heart is over there." She giggled as she leaned over him.

Aaron cupped her face in his hands. "My heart is right here." His lips curved as the distance between them diminished until Miriam was only a soft sigh away. "No kittens, no *kinner*. I might not be able to do this on my own," he whispered.

She smiled. "I think you've been on your own long enough. I think it's time you came home."

And when he kissed her, Aaron knew he finally was.

# *Epilogue*

"This is against the rules, you know. Of course, that's something you're well familiar with." Bishop Weaver glared at Aaron.

Aaron wasn't surprised at the man's irritation. Although he'd allowed it, the bishop hadn't been thrilled with Aaron's involvement with the authorities in the past month. However, a recent visit from the sheriff, sharing how much the department appreciated the district's cooperation in putting a menace in jail, went a long way toward mollifying the old man. Aaron would never be mentioned in particular, as that might make him *hochmut*, and pride was contrary to their beliefs. But everyone knew who was instrumental in stopping the car theft ring. Now that they were caught, the extensive evidence Aaron's coworker and some others in the gang were prepared to provide would ensure Blake remained in prison for some time.

Aaron rubbed a hand over his mouth, hiding his smile. "I know. But I can't get married until I'm baptized into the church. And I did take all the classes before, planning to get baptized the previous fall. I didn't know I'd be kicked by a horse and end up in the hospital getting my arm set instead of being baptized that morning."

The bishop frowned at him. "You can't wait until this fall to go through the regular classes?"

"We need to get married this summer." Aaron glanced significantly at Miriam's stomach. Bishop Weaver followed his gaze and paled.

The older man's throat bobbed in a hard swallow. "I'll talk to the other ministers and we'll see what can be done. As you mentioned, you've already gone through all the classes." His mouth pinched. "And there have been enough who've vouched for you that lead me to believe you'll find the necessary support to be allowed to become a member of the church. *If* you find it possible to learn to follow the rules by that time." With another fierce frown, he turned and fled into his house as fast as his gaunt frame could take him.

Aaron grunted when Miriam elbowed him, hard. "You let him believe I was going to have a *boppeli*."

Aaron snuck a quick kiss before she could elbow him again. "You are, someday I hope."

She blushed. "We don't really need to get married that soon." Leaving the bishop's porch, she headed toward the buggy, climbing into it before he could assist her—sitting on the left side, Aaron noted with amusement.

As soon as he was inside with the door slid shut, he pulled her into his arms. "I need to marry you that soon. Every day that I'm not your husband seems like an eternity."

"Good thing they're that long, then, as you've plenty to do now that you have a building to set up your shop."

Although her tone was tart, she settled sweetly into his embrace. Aaron pressed smiling lips against the blond hair he'd initially associated with a glare.

"Who would've figured I'd end up renting a building from Isaiah on the same farmstead where my *bruder* and his wife—my ex-girlfriend—rent a home?"

"Who would've figured that I'd end up with you?" she retorted.

"Once I really got to know you?" Cupping her face, he kissed her gently. "Me. I just had to break a few rules to do it."

\* \* \* \* \*

Dear Reader:

Thank you so much for choosing to read Miriam and Aaron's story!

When Aaron first appeared in Miller's Creek I wasn't sure what his path would be, or even if he'd show up again. When he appeared in the next book, I wasn't sure if he was hero material. In writing *Her Unlikely Amish Protector*, it reinforced for me that a hero, or heroine, can choose their path forward despite their back stories. Miriam faced a choice that would severely impact her future when she was willing to accept the love she thought she deserved because of something she'd done in the past. We all have back stories. They alone do not determine our future. Whatever your back story is, I sincerely hope for the very best in your future.

Thank you again for choosing to read the Miller's Creek stories from the heart of Wisconsin. To keep updated on what might be next, stop by jocelynmcclay.com or visit me on Facebook.

May God Bless You,
*Jocelyn McClay*